Prolog

C000161985

Twenty-nine year old geologist and surveyor, Len Berkowicz has everything to live for: a wonderful companion and a successful career working for a major oil exploration company when his career mentor and friend Eric Leighton decides to send him to a risk prone oil exploration project in the Golan Heights.

The story is told in first person by Len's post traumatic event namesake, Naim. Through his point of view, the story of life within the hot bed of Middle Eastern territorial politics unfolds with a deliberate loss of identity to blend into the region's people when hopes of a rescue gradually fade away, despite co-operation with the British secret service for information in exchange for a rescue.

Compromising choices are made when he has to join the local rebellion against the Syrian government's armed forces in order to survive in the heartland of 'jihad'. However, the cost of his choices measure up against him as his family are taken hostage by the Syrian army deep into the disputed Turkish territory of A'zaz. While narrowly escaping an attempt on his own life, he continues to fight with the rebels in the hope of rescuing his wife and new born child.

In his journey he assimilates the true nature of the 'holy war' through the eyes of his comrades, realising that a far more complicated and subtle 'game' played between the communist and capitalist powers on the ground.

After years of service to the rebellion, Naim gets the opportunity to attempt a rescue of his wife and child from the captured group of hostages who have since been moved from Azaz, deeper into the ruins of the Rawanda Kalesi in Kilis, Turkey. Would he succeed in his mission that seemed doomed right from its inception? Would his mentor Eric be able to face his own demons at the choices he made in sending his friend into the eye of this conflict?

Can those of us living in the West be able to keep the dust at bay on our home turf when we decimate every Arabian state to rubble?

'An Alternative Point of View' tries to touch upon the final question while the final conclusion remains bittersweet attempting to answer why some civilians, despite the dangers, travel across the Turkish border into the hellish war zone of Syria.

For Shoubhit, you are the future as our generation and the ones before are past their relevance now. For my family who have been supporting me every moment. For those whom I could not name in the recorded brutalities accidentally witnessed, your deaths are not in vain. I hope this is your story.

Contents

001 - A Necessary Recollection

A palpable rhythm ran through the people walking by me on Twelfth Street, the grey overcast day made the marble on the corporate office pillars look colder. I was looking forward to meeting my god-son at the Academy Records Store in New York City. Much like his mum I was expecting him to be scrimmaging through old records looking for a piece of sonic history. I remember this place from years ago when we came to visit Josh's father, Eric who had built an enviable collection from this very store, carefully collecting over the years. A decade ago this was the only place where we would drop by after a hard day's work and the attached coffee shop gave plenty of cause to sit down and check through the eclectic assortment of vinyl records.

Eric and Joan were part of the city's rising elite, socialising only with those who mattered on an 'A' list of celebrities, business men, senators and the like. Remarkable as it were, they chose me and my wife Sara as Josh's god parents. As often as Eric mentioned why, he would say 'it matters less who you are, what matters is what you would leave behind'. At the time it seemed he was referring to my work ethic which was fairly persistent to say the least. It meant he trusted me to do the right thing when the time came, regardless of the cost even if it was personal.

Regardless of the troubling circumstances I was meeting his son today, I wanted to be by Josh while this unexpected tragedy unfolded around him. Poor kid, he had no clue and neither did I expect Joan's death on the late morning news yesterday.

As I walked into the record store, I caught a glimpse of him at a section of the '70's records' stack, holding up Jim Morrison's American Prayer in his hands.

'I would hold on to it if I were you, only a few of those were ever pressed. Never re-pressed after its first release back in the seventies, they are special: words once spoken, never repeated.'

'Uncle Len', Josh gave me a hug. He reminded me much of his mother, it almost felt like a part of Joan had remained in her son though she herself had departed a day ago.

'How are you keeping, son? I thought I would never see you again. Your parents, I and Sara would spend hours here foraging for our favourite records here. She was an absolute fan of The Doors and look what you have in your hands without even knowing that little detail!'

'Mum would never talk about those days, she thought I was too young for this stuff but I was already listening to her collection these last few years without her realising it.'

The boy's smile gave way to a tear at the corner of his eye. He wasn't over the recent tragedy at home, I couldn't blame him. Neither was I prepared for what had happened ever since I managed to escape a painful fate and 'came back from the dead' as the British extraction team had put it.

'Yes, but I always knew you were so much like your mum when we saw you, little one. You and Joan are like two drops of water.'

'How did you manage to survive, uncle? We thought you had died in the siege at the oil fields. Dad had your obituary on the papers too! Wish you could meet mum, she was increasingly unwell and unhappy though she would always be there for me, smiling. I hardly see dad at home anymore. All this at the exact same time when you reappeared out of nowhere. Why haven't you brought Aunt Sara with you? Are you apart the way mum and dad were these last few years?'

Josh's innocent recollections opened a dam of tears within me, though I hardly showed them on the outside.

'Josh, there is something I need to tell you. I wanted to wait till you were older but we are running out of time.'

I was afraid of this pivotal decision of disclosing to him the truth but he had a right to know especially after what his father had done, which was nothing short of murder. Joan would have approved had she been here except she is not and neither is Sara.

At this time, a loud explosion rumbled a few streets down south of Fifth Street. There was a panic in the record store as people dropped everything and frantically lounged for the exit. Five years of being in the middle of the world's worst conflict had taught me that the sound was that of an explosive that was 'native made' in the country where I was abandoned for dead.

Unlike the others I felt a strange sense of calm and resourcefulness as I held Josh and pulled him towards the fire exit as we took our leave from the other end of the store. The streets were full of people pouring in from Fifth Street. There were a few quite ragged and bloodied in the bunch, screaming and coming towards us.

I looked at Josh's hands, he still held the record proudly titled 'American Prayer' and gave him a reassuring look, then pointed to the nearest NYC subway. We will hide there, war had taught me the safest place to be in an attack was in the trenches and the subway would be our trench for now.

'Am scared, Uncle, what is happening?' Josh was shaking with fear.

'The inevitable, Josh. Don't be alarmed, look at me, you are going to be fine, trust me.'

He looked at me incredulously as I took him into an abandoned ticket office. It appeared to him to be a bad idea when everyone seemed to run out of the subway exit but I knew better: this attack was just the beginning of a prolonged war aimed not at the political institutions of America but at its innocent civilian populace.

'This will be just fine, we will be here for a few hours at least until things get quieter above us.'

'What did you want to tell me, Uncle? Everything's changed since the day we knew you were found alive and returned to Britain. Were you involved in what's been happening in those Arabic states?'

'No, Josh. I came out of there without being on anyone's side except for the side that could have saved my family. What am about to tell you should have waited a few years but am not sure how long I have until your mother's secret stays with me as will your father's and my own.'

Multiple emotions of doubt, fear and anxiety ran through the boy's face and I felt sorry for him. It was a lot to take at this age for a teen raised as he was in New York. A stark contrast to the boys younger than him in the sandy dunes back where I was in the Syrian dictator's regime.
Those boy's back in the dunes would watch the government's cohorts cull the 'rebels' in front of them, turning the market sands thicker and a brighter crimson with every beheading taking in the reverberating chants of 'Allah O Akbar' for the blood thirsty mob.

Josh was far from those boys desensitized by violence, halfway around the world but even then this recollection could be too strong for him. Unavoidable and inevitable, I tried to recollect my thoughts and tell him the truth as unrest unfolded on the streets above us.

Initially I found it difficult to speak knowing not where to begin. I had to settle on telling him the story from the point of view of a man named Naim. One who weathered the challenges with only the will to survive with his resilient head held high, in hope of a better conclusion, a better point of view.

002 - The boy in the message

Twenty four hours in a day is perhaps the only common parameter in every one's lives and it takes an incredible amount of patience and the killer habit to reflect back at the end of the day on what you could have done better.

However, here is the single harsh truth that we try to ignore: Avoidance is like a slow poison, an 'ignorance is bliss' drug that gravitates you towards to your future state similar to one found in dementia patients. I almost felt this myself: That I was once someone's father, a husband and lover and yet do not realise or remember the single most important connection on each of those relationships. Almost as if I was in someone's book and the reader observes that lack of cognizance and knows every single vital detail that I can no more recall. I am an actor in someone's story and the one question in the reader's mind is: 'What happened to him?'

More relevant than the question was what I had become: a rebel with a cause. Around me for miles the wasteland, flat with ridges of sand and dust dotted with single and double storied windowless dwellings. The landscape is harsh to say the least: the hunger of this part of the world had not been vetted for a very long time, even the ground had crevices that opened up to claim the dead. We call this the 'ground' and young blood had been spilled today as the ground was being prepared for the burials of those who would not return to their mothers and fathers.

The White Helmets formed a quiet group as they brought down the bodies off their trucks. Evidently they were too late but no one blamed them and none spoke a word.

One of the blood splattered bags had a cell phone tied to it. The bag was about 4 feet long so it had to be a young kid.

'This belonged to the one in the bag, hold it.'

Ahmed handed me the cell phone from the bag, a cheap Blu Z3: the kind a father would give to his son in the city.

'Call me if you are afraid, I will wait until you return!'

The phone seemed to echo the father's words, only I could hear it.

I had to know: who was this little form wrapped in the blood soaked linen bag? How did his phone not get taken in a war-zone which gets by the internet blackout using these nifty devices? I opened the phone and checked for calls, pictures or the grainy videos in the phone.

Pictures of other children scavenging in the grocery stores of the destroyed city: smiling. They had found food within the rubble of the store's smashed doors. Done their family proud, almost. The pictures were taken by the boy as the other kids were far too young to fit the description of the yet unnamed young one in the blood soaked bag that lay beside me,

13

Then a grainy video in the phone as I skimmed through: this was taken today.

Somebody fairly tall than a child had recorded it: a frightened cowering child sat in his haunches looking down at the ground among what seemed like a few shuffling feet of men from the rival tribe. One touches his cheek and almost instantly slaps him, he strains away from the impact. Was this the young one, a young boy of eight, maybe nine years old?

'He is just a boy, by God's grace he will live! Keep away from him, point your guns away please!' someone pleaded in Arabic.

The video frame moves away from the child, other's move away too and one of the men, our enemy, tries to protect the kid. There is a clear view of the kid even as he is being shielded. This is the view from whoever was holding the phone, recording it all.

A look of hope brings back some colour to the kid's face, maybe the elders who are bigger and stronger than him are kind too. Just like in the tatty story books of the stories of noble heroes who rescued the weak, the women and the children. The books he must have read in his school last spring, before the war broke out.

Only too soon four quick shots are fired at the kid, the impact knocks him against the wall behind him. The one recording this rushes to the boy to find the four shots tear his scalp from the exit wound at the back of the head. Skin around the face pulled back partly over the half closed lifeless eyes due to the exit wounds as bright crimson life blood was wasted on the ground below his head. The debate to let live or die: it was over.

I handed the phone to Ahmed: 'We have to find them. This isn't war.'

'This is Syed's fourth son, his name is Fakher. The devil has possessed these infidels, Naim. For them to have done this to a child!'

'Am handing this to the White Helmets when they are back here tomorrow, maybe they can show this to the world. We need a little help, Ahmed. We need to call in our differences with the other clan and join hands.'

'For what, Naim? Do we know whose side they are on, leave that aside do you know whose side you are on? Love many but trust a few, my friend else we will end up being murdered by our own western allies. The brutal truth in this video will never get to the media unless the whole world wanted it to. No one knows. No one wants to know the truth even if you shoved it in front of their faces. It's just us; us against them.'

'We can't all leave this hell, Ahmed. Not all of us can and will make the journey over those dangerous waters.'

'That is why we fight... This is our home, no other place can be. Turn your back to this and we would just end up in a camp somewhere living in tents at the mercy of the West. This fight will kill us one way or the other, what's the hurry?'

Ahmed was right, we had known this for some time. No aid or humanitarian help would be coming from the West but guns were a different matter. Wars meant good business for the West, no side of the conflict disagreed with that.

Sadly, the fighting was to continue to the bitter end until nothing was left to fight for. Somehow I had to give the little hand protruding from the bloody bundle a gentle squeeze. I put the phone in his little hand and closed it. It was his, his father's and he would never want to part with it.

I looked back at the boy's hands, beautiful hands and soft as petals. A doctor's hands, maybe a musician's. So much like Omar's or Sara's for that matter. Missing sons cry out for their mothers in the darkness, daughters cry for their fathers who never return, brothers buried in the ground while their aging surviving family look on.

Syed and I had much in common today as I decided to stay with his young son in this difficult time while I heard Ahmed console the broken father.

003 - A Rebel's life

Today like most days in a rebel's life the day was fairly quiet, families of friends lived in little dark and damp shelters of what remained of their bombarded homes in this corner of the city. Ragged mountains on the far western side of the land gave a vantage point to the army on the ground, always on the move to try and take possession of our precious freedom.

Most of my comrades were ordinary civilians running small businesses selling basic electrical items, clothes and farm machines and we even had an alcohol store back then. Always a myriad of colours in peace time, the village fair around the south-west where the 'burial ground' is now would be resplendent with the sounds of the Mizwad and the odd Sagat.

'Naim, will you settle for my water pump and sell me your cigarette lighter? You can forget your water shortages forever with this trusty little marvel!'

Ali would often try to acquire my lighter, the one I kept with me since my days spent working between New York and London. It was a gift from Sara, my wife of what now increasingly seemed from another life, one that now seemed like a distant dream, a far cry from my life now in the desert.

'No Ali, not in my life I wouldn't sell it. But I will buy your trusty marvel of a broken water pump, fix it and sell it back to you!'

All of us would join up laughing, much to the deep chagrin of our 'honest' Ali, who huffed and puffed in indignation and walked away with the machine in tow.

Those days were long gone, Ali had disappeared when the war started. We didn't for once believe that he escaped, he was too guileless to be able to escape. Ahmed would often speak about him and his follies with such fervour it would make me laugh until I cried.

I let that memory in for a brief second before turning the safety of my M16 rifle off as we quietly approached the dark and desolate temple ruins. Distant scattered assault fire set the dark fabric of the night on fire, the tracer bullets dancing in the night sky before they settled on their target.

Ahmed waved in the direction of the target which was our 'rescue' mission tonight, a mile up in the eastern face of the mountain. Profusely sweating after a furtive belly crawl across the plains from across the village, we could not risk detection or more lives tonight. We had to continue in the exact same way uphill.

Ahmed's eyes clouded with uncertainty as did mine: saving the rendezvous point was impossible, why did the elders give us this challenge?

The rendezvous was the focal point of relentless shelling from the army, there was very little resistance to the relentless shelling on the shelter. Decimation seemed complete as the shrapnel attempted to clean off the area around it in the same manner as a jet wash attempts to wash dirt off a paved road. It was a clean-up operation.

About two hours later, the five young rebels in my group slowly whittled down to three as we tried to advance across the difficult terrain. The continued shelling and firing had temporarily deafened us so we communicated with hand signs. My departed comrades were shot as they attempted to advance to vantage positions to access the focal point of the shelling.

What weighed down heavily on me at this time were their manner of dying and the fact that I could not remember their names: there were many fighters in this holy war. It wasn't always like this: I did remember my comrade's names when the war began but after five years of relentless fighting and watching them die with me, the whole purpose of that human connection seemed lost. So many had come and gone, so many yet to come and go. I wasn't sure what was worse: watching them die as I somehow managed to survive or the thought of me dying in action.

Ahmed had survived as I did and he was my only connection to being human. We both knew the feeling of surviving this conflict, just one feeling: our end does not come tonight. My departed comrades were much younger: we found the young teen who had caught a ricocheting bullet off a rocky ledge. As we slowly walked over to his wounded body, the poor soul's feet were twitching almost childlike. Like a toddler wiggling his feet before he fell asleep in his comfortable bed. Ahmed read my mind and shot the boy in the head to release his trapped soul and read a prayer.

'Rest in your mother's arms, Youcef. Play with her and pray that you come back to this land in better times when it awaits you with open arms!'

'Ahmed, his last moments what do you think he was thinking of? His legs were twitching like I would if I jumped onto a comfortable bed. We just took that illusion away from him or did we deliver him to the lord?'

Ahmed's voice was choking with emotion as he delivered his comrade.

'The truth is there is no comfortable bed for him, Naim. Not in this life anyway.'

Unlike me, Ahmed could never quite cope with a loss of his comrade. Each loss brought out a brighter nobility in my friend that strengthened his inner resolve to fight for the good of his land and protect what mattered the most: the legacy of the people left behind in this city. Unlike me he still remembered their names long after they were gone.

004 – Mission Ambushed

As the three of us crawled ahead Ahmed motioned us to stop, indicating to the east point of our destination which was not covered by the firing artillery and the tanks. This meant we would have to cover higher ground to make it to sub machine guns at the rendezvous point which were mostly lifeless returning sporadic retaliatory fire from a lone assault rifle. The rendezvous point was at risk of being overpowered by the powerful shelling directed at its centre.

My observation was cut short when a few tracer bullets caught fire above us on the dry desert bushes: Ahmed was already on to higher ground, he needed cover. Reloading my M16, I motioned the other two to follow my lead as I poured bullets into the armour guns in the distance. While I had armour piercing rounds this only had a temporary effect of pausing the armoured gun's attack as my bullets met a few casualties briefly taking the attention off my friend.

Like a horde of bees finding a new target, within a split second the army's shell and shrapnel found us above our heads. We dropped back on the ground but kept up a furious pace on our belly crawl towards Ahmed. Our hands trembled, sweat poured off our backs and our necks hurt but not one dared to get up at the risk of being shot. Our heads pinned to the ground, I could not but help find the earth and dirt on the ground smell sweet while the air above us reeked with the acrid smell of gunpowder.

Ahmed managed to sprint the last leg of our approach to one of the sub machine guns. For a brief moment as the army realized of a presence within the sub machine guns, the action paused if only for a second as the rendezvous point mounted its defence.

The pause broke with Ahmed's grand firing at the three armoured guns about five hundred metres away. Two of the guns caught fire, the third one had stopped. Just the two tanks advancing from the western end had to be neutralised as they rolled slowly within the same distance as the now quiet armoured guns.

Picking the RPG launcher and shell off the back of a new recruit, I primed the weapon to fire at one of the tanks turning its menacing singular attention at the rendezvous point.

انتظر! (IntaZara'!)

The boy started to speak, his words cut off by a rifle bullet from behind the third armour gun: Ahmed had not neutralised his third target.

For a moment, the advancing tank had stopped, almost as if sensing that it was being watched and aimed at. It blew up before it could prepare its next manoeuvre as I rendered it useless. Ahmed neutralised whatever came off it and he was closing his account on the third armour gun. We would not give up tonight's mission: too many of us lost our lives getting this far.

At this unexpected turn of fortune, the army started to withdraw to assess the damage, the battlefield fell silent except for the engines of the retreating tanks. The battle paused for a few minutes, this was our only window to check the rendezvous point and retreat.

As the boiling mercury of the ambush settled, I realised the recruit had survived and walked over to him as my frustration boiled over at his attempted bravado.

'You are flesh and blood, Parvez. It would be fatal to consider otherwise and it would be safe to set aside the notion of a heroic martyrdom for the commendation in Allah's court or to expect the promise of his virgins!'

We rushed over to where Ahmed was crouched close to the sub machine guns witnessing an astonishing sight: an army soldier lay on the dry sand, his blood darkened the sand around his body. A split shrapnel had shredded his spleen draining onto the sand that was turning a dark crimson under him. He didn't have much time left, behind the bunker were a cowering family of five, riddled with bullets.

Once a family of six, the father a proud major of the army complete with his stripes sat in the centre of his family. Now his young wife and children lay slaughtered behind him, the youngest holding onto to his mother's chest.
The little boy, closest to his mother, riddled with bullets so bad we only could make out an infant form. The mother still had her dignity, her veil in place. A bullet through her baby's back took rest in her bleeding heart. That would have killed them almost simultaneously. No mother should have to watch her baby die this way and so I thought that God is merciful.

The major was close to making his inevitable journey himself. A proud major, a divided family over the principles of the conflict and this was the inevitable tragic end.

"Inna lillahi wa inna ilayhi raji'un!"
Ahmed didn't know who they were, neither did we but his prayer was all that mattered to these defenceless bodies left in undignified slaughter.

None of us spoke, every mission out here to the heights would claim one from the team. The dead weighed heavily on our minds for a while, telling us in many unspoken words of their desire to have lived a little longer. Then they went away, disappearing into the next day's dawn in lament realising the futility of holding on hence preparing for the ultimate inevitable journey.

The wounded soldier broke our reverie not so more with his constant intense yet peaceful gaze at our faces: he didn't have much time left, yet it seemed he wanted to share his last secret with us.

Ahmed went over to him, leaned over on his haunches. The major didn't have a shred of emotion on his face though he was slipping away as the rest. Squinting in dawn's daylight which shone behind Ahmed, he reached feebly for a photo in his pocket.
We saw the picture and it was quite clear why the soldier was caught on the other side of his own army's gunfire.

Once a loyal major, now a devoted father came back to protect what mattered the most: family. However, the major was but a number, a pawn in the army while the father was all and one in his family. Both lost to the conflict that now divided several families in the hills.

A sickening feeling filled me from inside, a deja vu that I always ran away from.

"Hal tasheur bial'alam?" I asked him, contemplating taking him out of his misery if he was in pain.

The dying major took my hand and gave me the picture, it was dear to him and smiled as he finally slipped away. Did he know his exact moment of death? Why did he seem to be in a better place than I am right now?

The mission was a failure. The elders had sent us to protect this man and his family. We know now why: he was the enemy's army major who was willing to give us information in exchange for protection of his family, though what that information was we were yet to know. Was it worth even trying to imagine a life of freedom at the risk of endangering your own family?

The question did not leave my thoughts as we made the most of the time left for us to make our way back to the base of the hills before the sun laid bare our way back to the camp.

The sight of the slain family with the bleeding major stayed within me. My thoughts returned to my own family. I had lost them to circumstances beyond my control but not forever I hope. I will find them, hold them and love them and I hope they will understand why I am here, what am about to do. The three of us will stand one day and look into a picture framed and viewed by others. Just as the family picture of the proud army major who swore to protect the people of this land and died today with honour. I wondered what Sara, Omar and I would look like as a family and found it hard to visualise as it had been five long years. The thought itself made me feel vulnerable as I steadied myself looking into the dark horizon for a safe way back to the base.

005 - Innofuel's Finest

Truth had a habit of filtering through the most censorial of filters and despite the most flagrant manner of bowdlerization they eventually get to the general public: the truth around brutal war crimes, genocide and the role of the West in both.

This was the era of fake news dropped on unsuspecting civilians where the principle of truth is a mere topicality. Withholding truth is powerful and the world's strongest governments exercise this with impunity which is ironic considering the copious sources of genuine information available on the internet.

Paper Journalism had to die when the net gave us the access to 'near real time' news. Recorded video posted on websites around the globe from a first person point of view turned us into voyeurs for violence. Those who stumbled across these recorded brutalities were aware of the plight of hundreds in the eye of the Arab Springs. To them it added a distorted dimension to their entertainment, a voyeuristic insight in to inflicted cruelty.

Humans have always been drawn to depictions of torture, horror and pain. Our museums and exhibits help us relive those emotions. Our admission ticket to view the spectacle is not the price we pay to view them but to desensitize ourselves to the world around us, to accept it and live happily in denial. The purpose of the net despite its power and importance is lost in the desire to be a voyeur to the experience of pain.

Eric always made light of the fact that the censorship was in place to keep the average man from deciding to act, that the whole idea behind not showing grotesque war imagery on the internet or the television was to protect 'the children of the future' from losing their innocence early on. Neither did he believe that the censorship was in place to keep the people 'in control', as some conspiracy theorists would say.

Eric reasoned with the genuine truth that people in general had just got lazy to correlate facts together to decide what was true and what was not. Most of us just depended on someone on the news channel to tell us what was a 'ruthless genocide', a 'fact' in Eric's glossary and the deduction on who perpetrated the act was the accompanying body of 'fiction'. It was quite evident that Eric loved reading up the facts and draw deductions of his own.

He was a realist besides his scrupulous ambition for power and wealth in a business which welcomed men of his kind: oil. In Eric's rule book, if the exposition of a fact would not make a difference to an ordinary person's choices in life it was better not to hand him the facts. What was the point after all in showing the brazen violence of conflict while all one worried about was the mortgage, the bills and getting by in life in general? There was no time to contemplate such information in today's modern schism of 'I, Me and Myself'?

'Half of this world's children watch someone they know, someone they love being brutally terminated in front of an audience be it a beheading or a public execution either on a shared video or first hand. Innocence lost much early on', Eric spoke to his wife and continued.

'There is but one and only one need that drives all nature of conflict in the last two centuries: Natural resource such as Oil, Gas or both. Russia is the only country which exports more of gas than it imports, our stars and stripes hardly export but we cannot keep our hands off unexplored black gold. Especially in the Middle East, add a dash of ordnance revenue primed off the various conflicts and we are warm and happy!'

'And the children from this half of the world just get to worry about outdoing everyone else on the things they have, it's not fair. Eric, am afraid this will come full circle, ending where it started, right here', Eric's wife replied with an irony in her voice. It was a sombre reflective rejoinder to his opportunistic thoughts, clashing dramatically as fire and ice.

Eric wondered if Joan could read his thoughts with these vocal rejoinders: it was uncanny but in the two decades of being together he had realised many a times that Joan was indeed thinking on the same wavelength as him without his saying a word. And neither ever acknowledged the fact either, theirs was an unspoken bond in the concurrence of their thoughts.

However, his thoughts never moved too far from the delicate fate of the oil fields of the Rumeilan region: for far too long had the federation waited to get some control of the oil fields it inadvertently destroyed almost a decade ago.

The war had been on for nearly a decade now and the graphic images on the news which provoked Joan's reaction was merely to stir the general public to support the federal objective of decimating the opposition at these oilfields with whatever force necessary.

Eric took a deep breath in, turned his gaze to his laptop showing a real time analytic on the price of black gold per barrel as the latest defeat of the rogue president's army advances unfolded over the news. The slight rise in the barrel prices gave a glimmer of hope.

News of brutalities from the Middle East were like echoes of radio pings lost in space: they have always been there but they keep echoing until after someone heard them out or transmitted them.
We were just tuning in as the syndicate decided to mould the public opinion before the decision to decimate the country with its citizens would be justified as 'necessary collateral' to regain control over the oil fields.

'They are getting really impatient this time', he thought as the news showed more and more graphic details of the communist backed leader's atrocity on its defenceless civilians injured in hospitals only to be further firebombed with chlorine and mustard gas.

The war had given Eric plenty to live by although he feebly wrestled, lost and somehow survived with the moral implications of his position as CEO of the world's foremost oil and natural resources company, InnoFuel. He couldn't care less if the West instigated a fake attack on the hapless countries to justify taking control of their natural resources, effectively clearing the path for Innofuel to prepare for oil exploration, or rather, extraction. It was better this way as it deterred the OPEC from pushing the barrel prices higher. That was the silver lining that kept him going, besides his ambition.

However, it had been a good end to a Sunday evening for him. Somewhere, in close proximity to the oil fields a group of valiant rebels had fought off an army offensive on tanks and the advance to the oil fields had paused.

Whether they lost their men or felt anguish as they saw their enemy's eyes fill up with the same didn't matter: Oil Prices were buoyant as he had predicted and it was going to be a very satisfying start to the week tomorrow on Monday morning.

006 - The cog in the wheel

Sitting in a windowless MI5 office on Cannon Street with its high ceiling, Sam completed a quick mental review of the wood effect wall mural set around the floor: urban chic, not too distracting. It was the window, or the lack of it that was distracting.

This was his new desk at the windowless corner, it had low partitions across to another desk. After months of renovation and an unavoidable relocation, he already disliked its tepid outlook.

Down under a pile of files was the one piece of paper he had been avoiding looking at all morning: it was a minute of a meeting tracking the destruction of a vital pipeline link close to Aleppo. The very fate of the world's oil economy depended on its existence. The pipeline, no longer in active operation was getting destroyed by the incessant war and bombing by the local army: they had to be stopped.

However, this is where the battle lines weren't clear and the West's interests could not be deemed entirely ethical. There were no heroes here, only role players at the expense of the innocent civilians who had no wish to partake in the savage violence.

The not so unfamiliar emotion brought an itch to his throat: he needed a smoke.

Mid-march afternoon on a busy day on Cannon Street: you

could be here on your own, thoughtfully smoking away and completely invisible from the people rushing past you. Standing at the rear end of his office lobby, Sam inhaled sharply on his cigarette, the reassuring smoke filling his lungs completely. He felt consoled, almost as if someone patted his back like a good friend.

'It isn't as bad as it seems, Sam.'
Sam looked over to the voice on the right: it was Dave, the fastidious business analyst, his colleague and friend for now well over a decade.

'You been out here for long or did you just sneak upon me?', he asked Dave looking away, taking the view of the Thames from the embankment. Sam wanted to know if Dave could skim the thoughts off his face, after all they did talk about 'the plan' a few days ago.

'Am always out here even when I am inside, you know. All this fresh air and you had to get smoky, you son a bitch. Look down there at those lovely people walking by the Parliament. They love them buildings, don't they? Those houses of parliament stand for democracy, Sam. Tourists come to see them every day, take a few pictures of themselves facing off the Eye. Cheer up, there is life out here even if there is war out there. No one cares if they don't see the pain first hand that is for us to see and interpret! See how I stress 'interpret', Sam?'

Sam shrugged his shoulders, took the cigarette in his hand and blew the smoke by his left, avoiding Dave's glance. He had to be sure of what was in his friend's mind.

'How long we have been here, Dave? One of the nameless

hundreds in the department? How long has it been? A Decade? What is left for us to know or do not know that we can't make a difference to? We took this job because we thought we could bring about change. The job has changed us, Dave. Naim could still be out there fighting for his life and here we are holding the key to his survival. How powerful is that?'

'It still cannot be done, Sam: the idea is brilliant but unreal. I am an everyday bloke with mortgage, loans and a decrepit line of credit and need this time to stabilise into the 'nice guy' image I once had. You need to get your act together after your refusal to give up those Muslim families to our departmental Islamophobes! All eyes are sharply on us, you know the situation is unreal, Sam. Short of being called terrorists we are the most hated in our department!'
Dave inhaled sharply, trapping the smoke from his cigarette in his chest till he felt the warmth inside.

A cold unsettling feeling of doubt crept into Sam's heart which he promptly dismissed with another sharp intake from his cigarette: Dave was right, the 'plan' was unreal though not entirely impossible. But to Sam it was necessary, he would go down with the 'plan' alone if he could.

But even in his heart Sam knew he needed a team. The 'plan' had to be a team effort: it was bigger than him or Dave. This was about saving lives that had been ignored for far too long in the eye of the Arab springs. Both of them were aware that a British National with no knowledge in the matters of the conflict was pulled into its maelstrom of violence yet had survived practically unscathed. The story was circulating within the office much like a heart-warming rumour but only Sam and Dave knew that it was indeed true.

Sam exhaled slowly as he realised the overwhelming scale of what they had planned. He needed a team and he needed to go through the details meticulously once again before attempting to deploy an isolated extraction rescue by elite extraction units.
He glanced at the time on his wristwatch, nodded at Dave and went inside back to his windowless desk: There was work to do.

007 - A part of me

In some dark subconscious corner of our mind resides the warmest memories we hold dear. Like a most amiable nameless friend they would come in my dreams showing snapshots of me with my family in a different time: I didn't always live in this village.

I was in London, walking into Chinatown with Sara, my wife haranguing about which restaurant to walk into for our special weekend dinner.

Long boring missives about which of these had the best 'dim sum' usually met with a shrill 'Whatever' from my wife echoed with equal indignation. These wonderful moments on the streets of Soho's Chinatown on a chilly winter night could go on forever.
We finally settled on the exotic though exorbitant Yauatcha restaurant and I still remember her handing me a note and asked me to read it to her. The details do escape me for the most but I could still remember in parts on what I had written on that note in an apparent hasty scrawl:

'One can spend nights and days wondering how to start writing out consistently the fleeting thoughts in one's mind. To begin writing is possibly the toughest part of process and it is quite similar to social conversations aimed to 'break the ice'. The beginning almost always tends to be awkward even if we love the euphoric sensation of a great beginning. To be able to make the best beginnings is to then write on the subject closest to your heart: that I was an economic migrant and had come over to Britain to live an honest man's living.

Every migrant having made that journey has a story to tell on the challenge to their own beliefs in the country which they have chosen to make their own. I like to make sure that mine story would be unique to keep you hooked from the first page that you will be transfixed and every nuance of my intended expression will move you, enchant you?

I should have no such grand ambitions so I will try to deal with a paradox on the definition of the 'exotic'.

If this confuses you, please accept my apologies: My father would often say that those who visit Israel from the West deem everything that they experience as 'exotic'. Taking a dip in the Dead Sea is exotic, sitting across the sea caked in the medicinal sea mud is exotic. So much of its people's suffering seemed lost in the heady boom of tourism in his home town of Tel Aviv.

Strange then, what is an outsider in the grey cosmopolitan city of London to think of as exotic? The cheerful bustle of city life, the chilling breeze across the Thames, the endless energy and ambition of its citizens, maybe all of it is. Sitting across my dinner looking at Sara's eyes, I catch a glimpse of the reflection in front of me whom I had stopped paying attention for too long a time.

True, twenty four years have passed since I last remember when life was not a blur to this point when I can choose not to just speed by as a blur. So much has changed. We have all grown up and each of our lives are worth re-telling to many others for sure but I am going to stick to just one story. A story of an 'alien', a 'migrant' who is more at home in this land then he ever was in his home land. Nothing new in that premise save for the fact that it is probably not just my story but of many others who are either too tired to write, do not wish to emote or just won't express but will surely smile when they read this and on. This does resonate somewhere within someone surely.

For the story to begin of the 'alien', it must begin from where he originally came from and why did he end up being an economic migrant. Why are countries around the world seeing a trend of people migrating into Europe even when the journey across the treacherous waters seemed less promising?

This story must begin from the little boy who would stare wide eyed at his dad's turntable as it played a 45: what is that black circle spinning with a needle touching the surface? How was it playing that wonderful song from the white ceramic platter? Who is this boy going to grow up to be? What is his story?'

I was surprised that this scrawl still existed while I had forgotten about it.

'Where did you find this? My first bit of writing, I thought I had lost it a long time ago. You had this all the time?'

She replied with just the bit of sarcasm that made me notice: 'That scrawl was you writing such wonderful paragraphs in the hope of starting a writing project and then just drop it. Len, when will you ever finish what you started? It's just gross to begin on such grand notes and then deciding to let go of the idea altogether!'

It did make me think though: I had a job that kept me occupied for most of my waking hours as a geological 'on site' consultant for an oil and gas exploration company. There was just as much time to focus on anything else, leave alone a writing project. But somewhere within me there was a voice which did rebuke me to try to be someone else, someone far bigger and stronger than I was. I mistook this for my ambition until at some point following my ambitions did not give me enough satisfaction. Maybe following my dreams would cure me from my dull stupor that made one day increasingly indistinguishable from the other.

The nice Chinese gentleman broke my reverie when he gave us the set menu options for the best dim-sum in this part of London. Within minutes, we are greeted with the wonderful aroma of dumplings beautifully arranged on a plate and we heartily tuck in. This wonderful memory freezes into a picture frame. I realise I am not in the restaurant, the man whom I thought I am was no more than a mere recollection from a past long forgotten.

I am in a different time frame, in a different part of the world and this entire conversation seemed now too distant, almost unreal in the current circumstances. Len was history and Naim had taken over as ideals gave way to realism and the sandy wind blew strongly over the dunes to obscure my past.

I wake up to Ahmed shaking my shoulder, gently urging me to wake up in hushed tones: 'Naim! Wake up, time to head back to the camp!'

Nodding as I shook my dreams off my head, my present circumstances hit me as boiling water on gentle hands: in the desert, laden with grit and my sweat now giving a stench from weeks of wearing damp khaki borrowed from the resistance.

I felt my spirit quiver at the thought of how circumstances have changed but I urged my mind to stay calm and steady, reminding why I am here in the desert instead of my comfortable life back in. We needed to move out of the hills before sunrise to get to the base before the enemy's rifles found us.

008 - The Ordnance map

"Do you remember them often, Naim?"

Ahmed's question would linger and stay for much longer in the crevices of my heart, long after he himself had forgotten the question. The dry summer dirt beneath my bare feet would seem to cry out for more blood, its hunger seemed to rise with the summer heat during the day and transformed into a cool contrite sinner by nightfall. As the ground seemed to yaw beneath my feet, I felt as if it would try to claim me, dragging me underneath. Hastily I put my shoes on and got up on my feet, summoning the others to resume the journey back to the elders.

Staying calm was never in my nature but I had trained my mind, to keep my 'mindscape' in order despite the fact that the world around us sunk a little more into the dusty rubble. The resolve helped immensely in times when our little resistance groups lost their men to an abrupt end and I had to recon on their behalf to get them back to base safely. It was an invaluable lesson from Ahmed to pray and calm the mind, or the 'mindscape' as he would call it, an obvious pun on the remotely sonant synonym: 'landscape'.

Ahmed had been keeping a secret since the ambush ended and I could tell from his clenched fists and knitted brow.

'What is it, Ahmed? You haven't spoken a word since we left the barracks. We have a ten mile hike ahead of us and you have never been this quiet this long. If you are considering the mission a failure, don't. We did our best for a man and his family who were but a magnet for tanks and machine guns. There was nothing we could do!'

"Our mission was not the man and his family at the barracks, He was an army lieutenant so why would the elders send us to rescue him? Yet he was being hunted by the same army to which he belonged. Why do you think? He was a traitor to the army but a martyr to his country. What a contradiction it is then that he chose to give his life for information that is irrelevant to most but is gold to those who need it!"

Ahmed was lost in thought while he procured a ragged scroll which was slightly soiled due to dust and age from his breast pocket, then continued:
"I took an ordnance map off his hands when he motioned me to show him his family's photo at the time."

The unusual mention of an ordnance map broke my reverie bringing back among a feeling of curiosity, a familiarity to the object, that mention of an ordnance map, would bring within me. I had made, read and interpreted ordnance maps before.

However, the point being Ahmed's mention of an ordnance map in the hands of the dying lieutenant. The intrigue as well as the familiarity of the words 'ordnance map' shattered my 'mindscape'.

"An ordnance map? You mean like a survey map? Where is it and why didn't you tell me earlier? Let's have a look, come on.'

This was not ordinary, and could not be just a coincidence: an army general, with an ordnance map being shot down by the very same army along with his family? This had me thinking, it also had me worried that the elders had us involved in a mission far beyond our understanding: This was bigger than either of us.

"An Ordnance Survey Map? Why would he have one on him---", I was too drawn into drawing the dots now.

Ahmed unfolded the ordnance map which grew from a 5 inch by 6 inch tenfold to a large map that looked similar to the eastern end of the foothills close to the village. Almost immediately I realised that why the map didn't show the same geography as I knew of the foothills, it showed what seemed like oil and natural gas reserves under the area that could sustain prosperity in the village for several decades. The map however lacked the official seal of the government making it appear as some expert's unofficial and as yet unverified map of the resources beneath our land.

"Ahmed, the map is older than the regime, drawn before the siege began. If this is what the elders were after, what would be our fate now that we know about this map? This is treasure for those who are powerful enough to dig for oil and pump through pipelines or using trucks. This is a find our elders cannot use though they could auction this to the highest bidder for a price."

"The rescue mission was the map and not the lieutenant or his slaughtered family! La haula wa la quwwata---those innocent children riddled with bullets for this? So we are the same as the greedy regime, selling our land to those who bid the highest! I don't want to believe this, Naim! This was not our war, this is not the cause! I have no family save for you to call my brother, what difference would selling this information make to me? I joined Mahmud because I believed in his noble intention of bringing the village back to the villagers!"

"Our country is not ours anymore, Ahmed, it is for those who come to take it. Our clan was never recognised when the government was formed, we were driven out into the lands of drought. Our crops died, our livestock followed. Our elders seek the help of the Islamic Caliphate who shower us with meagre gifts of food and water that help us survive. And the one commodity that will keep those gifts coming is information. The value of the information ensures we get what we need to continue our fight. We have to take their help, Ahmed else we won't survive!"

"The Caliphate are our brothers, our heroes! How can you speak of them with less reverence? After all the support we have from them in holding off the army?"

"Not with less reverence, Ahmed, with caution: If this map was our mission, it was never intended to reach the army and it obviously is not intended to reach the western powers considering the Caliphate's hatred for the West. This was meant for the one power who are backing the army at the moment: the communist regime. They handpicked the lieutenant knowing his allegiance to our group, the elders arranged the escape. We were sent to extract him and his family, in exchange for this map."

"A failed escape! Were the dead children part of this plan too? We weren't supposed to know this. How did you know this was an ordnance map? You surprise me, Naim, call me 'your' best friend yet I know nothing of what you know, you sly jackal."

"Would you question the Caliphate? Considering all the help the elders get through them? The Caliphate were in Kabara when your uncle went to trade his ram. How I wish to meet your only family but he never returned, did he? No one claims to have seen him since neither he was found. That was two years ago, still no signs of Haider being alive! There are no heroes here, no honour in the eyes of Allah or the reward of a thousand virgins. We are still here, fighting the 'holy' war as foot soldiers. The Caliphate says we are winning. Do you feel like you are winning, Ahmed?'

The criticism brought tears to Ahmed's eyes but he would cry only when we were alone lest someone considered him to be weak. Ahmed's secret was painful, he had an uncle who went one dry unforgivably hot day towards the market sands where he lived to sell his last livestock: an old ram. Haider, his uncle never came back. For days Ahmed waited, looking at the horizon with moist eyes waiting to catch a glimpse of his silhouette. After about six months he gave up and left his hometown in Africa to come over to be with his distant uncle, Mahmud. He concluded that no one went away that long to sell an aging ram. But the question burnt into his conscious through the years like a festering wound: What happened to Uncle Haider?

The journey to the market sands was about twenty five miles, mostly through the desert. Haider thought this over at least once every passing day: On a blistering hot summer as this, it would take two days to walk to the market sands with a bottle of precious water and an assortment of dried fruits on his own. With Hamid in tow, it would take an additional day to get there as he wasn't sure if Hamid could walk all the way given his age and health.

Hamid was Haider's healthiest ram in happier times, when the rain would blow into the village in time for the crops to mature for harvesting in autumn. All that changed in the last decade when the desert started to expand into the city and the rains got more erratic. The crops dried before they matured and rotted in the fields as the sand blew in from the ever expanding desert over the northern edge of the African continent. They called it 'global warming'.

Apparently, Haider's, the people in his village or their fore-fathers had nothing to do with it. Their own simple ways of living had nothing to do with the slow and sure decimation of the delicate environment but the winds of change were blowing in from the West.

'The Western countries go to great extent to keep their cities clean for their health and happiness, yet they do not think twice about dumping ready to eat food in the oceans instead of feeding it to the poor! Why? Because it is just not feasible for the West to do so! Same goes for all the industrial manufacturers, they won't stop choking the sky even if it meant destroying the planet.

It is us who will have to remind them, to make them understand what they are doing over there is affecting our lives around here!'

Ahmed's detailed missive greatly pleased Haider, after all the sacrifices he had made for educating this bright young boy.
His main source of all information was Ahmed, his nephew, who would enthral wide eyed villagers with his knowledge of how the 'West' has been instrumental in bringing about the winds of climactic change.

"Climactic change has nothing to do with us who are living our lives by the rites of the Holy Quran! This climactic change is what is bringing the northern desert to our doorstep! While the West keeps increasing their factories and poison the air, who does it affect the most? Us! Despite us living our lives by the Quran, we are nothing but goats to slaughter for the Western countries!"

Though a large part of his rapt audience did not fully understand Ahmed's discourses, they did admire the young chap's knowledge and respect for his own kind. They also sized up the 'West' as some seemingly large ominous monolith sucking up all that makes the earth good. They despised this 'Western civilisation' passionately and scoffed at the sarcasm in Ahmed's voice.

Haider knew Ahmed was right though he himself could not connect the dots. But he did notice the changing of the seasons, he heard about the 'greenhouse' emissions on the radio, he even felt the change of the winds along the river which was reduced to a stream now. Where did all the water go? In less than a decade half his livestock had died due to starvation, some of his livestock were even butchered by hungry orphaned children who had but one determination and that was to survive. He had managed to sell a few of them for Ahmed's education, for his text books, pens and copy books but he had no money left. Hamid was his last attempt to provide for his beloved nephew whose mother and father had been taken away by the government army across the village borders.

Haider never had the heart to tell Ahmed that his parents had been decapitated, severed by their heads alive and dumped into a common grave while some were crucified with crude nails and then burnt alive.
He had seen the killing fields from a distance and heard the screams, each one of which he could identify a name and a face. The unmistakable smell of burning flesh as it blackened against the heat of the raging fires was engraved into his memory. Haider tried to be optimistic despite this knowledge of their terrifying end and looked with quiet apprehension as the Caliphate defended their village from the army's further incursions.

"We are farmers, we are not comfortable with guns and bullets above our heads, whichever side they may come from!", he thought.

Hamid, his ram was his last hope of getting some money for Ahmed's books and some food supplies. Yes, Hamid was healthy but the years of drought reduced every patch of vegetation edible to the ram to dust. Hunger and starvation was rapidly aging the poor animal. Haider had hoped that the droughts would end sooner than later. In his heart, he really wished that Allah was protecting all good folks like them and that this was really a short test, nothing more. That this 'global warming' would stop in its heels and God himself would set things right.

'Allah loves us, Hamid. He is just testing our virtue, our strength. Tests end and then come the rewards which we will surely reap. You will see, then Ahmed will complete his studies and you will feed on the finest, juiciest grass in all of Timbuktu!'

He fed Hamid tufts of wild grass, mixed with dried hay. Hamid, his beloved ram he would never part with, until now. It was time for the journey to the market sands. Haider never believed it would come to this that he would have to part with his dear ram whose horns he wrestled in happier times, whose long ears he used to tweak and tease. The long years of drought, the relentless Tuaregs and the murderous caliphate ensured that business needed to be done elsewhere, in the market sands of Kabara.

010 - The long journey to the market sands - II

"Oh you, who go to Gao, make a detour by Timbuktu, murmur my name to friends and bring them the scented greeting of exile which sighs after the ground where his friends, his family, his neighbours reside."

Haider sang this in his head while preparing for the long journey to the market sands. It was a line from the ancient poems on one of the preserved manuscripts in the Ahmed Baba library and it gave him comfort, some hope that one day this part of the country will be whole again. The ever expanding Sahara was the one factor they had always learnt to live and cope with. Historically, Timbuktu had managed to survive disasters caused by man or nature. Surely then, this is just a phase?

Haider tied a light noose around Hamid's neck and gently urged the Ram to start the walk. In his left coat pocket, he kept 4 slices of home baked bread and a small box of pickled onions. In the right he carried a small water bag of cow hide and some dried fruits. The cow hide bottle was a necessity if one wants to keep the water cool for a long journey such as this.

'Ahmed, am off to the market sands! Hamid is coming with me this time but don't worry I will be back with enough money to last us this season. Don't forget to feed the chickens and don't leave them out in the night!'

After hugging Ahmed and reminding him to feed the remaining chickens in his backyard, Haider finally set off towards the desert sands close to the Niger, singing the same song in his heart.

'Uncle Haider, come back soon! Don't take days and days like last time. If Hamid comes back that's ok too but please do not be gone for as long as last time!'
Ahmed's words echoed in his mind as he set on the trail towards the market sands.

As he entered the sand and dust bowl, he realised the sands felt a lot sharper to the touch, almost needle like as his village reduced to a pale shadow behind him. The sun was beating down hot like the hammer on hot iron set upon an anvil. Haider looked at Hamid and he saw a slight hesitation in the ram's eyes.

"Hamid, am not going to give you to someone who would kill you, do you understand? There will be someone who would need a ram to till a vegetable patch in his garden. Some rich guy maybe, you will see! You will be fine, my friend."

Rams weren't quite like dogs: you never felt the affection instantly but you could feel it in the softening of their eyes. Hamid and Haider had grown fond of each other over the years like brothers, although one was man, his master and other was a ram. Hamid strode along bravely along the desert with his master, not for once doubting his master's words.

Soon the sun lost its intensity in the late afternoon, Haider thought this would be the best time to stop for a while. He picked the small rucksack off Hamid's back to take out some fresh grass and water: the ram carried his own lunch.

After setting up Hamid for lunch, Haider set out his own and scanned the horizon as he ate. Smoke rose off the southern side not so far from Kabara, accompanied by faint sounds of sniper shots 'Bok! Bok! Bok!' This rang warning bells
within Haider: Kabara was never a conflict zone between the Tuareg rebels and the government.

Squinting in the dying sun, Haider saw uniformed soldiers lined up by another group of armed militia. They weren't the Tuareg as none of them had the familiar flag of the Tuaregs. It was the ominous black flag of the Ansar Dine. His heart sank as this meant more delay going towards Kabara where the market sands were.
'Must wait until dark to decide whether to move ahead or risk being shot down!'
Haider spoke gently to the ram.

The hours passed by with a succession of shots fired at the rounded up soldiers after a fiery speech by the head of the militia addressed to his young recruits. With the day's discourse and execution complete, they filed out on trucks into the shimmering hot desert.
By late afternoon, army trucks came back for their fallen comrades as they filed into the same route taken earlier by the militia. Haider watched in despair as a full-fledged battle unfolded at night with tracer bullets hitting the Ansar Dine camps to the south west of Kabara. Half a day's travel had been disrupted and this meant lesser food rations for him and even worse, lesser food for Hamid.

Hamid had to be kept fed till he was sold, no one would buy an impoverished ram if it looked like a bag of bones. Haider fed Hamid as much as he could but the ram was getting older and seemed to have gained some human wisdom from his own master. The ram did not know the nature of the conflict but of late Hamid did seem increasingly depressed when he heard distant gunshots or picked up sounds of civil strife on the streets. Haider hugged him, patting him, cajoling him to sleep.

Morning came and Haider broke out of his sleep with a start: the firing had stopped, a huge fire raged from the Ansar Dine camps. This time the victory was with the army and the path looked clear.

"Blessed am I, Lord! Get up, Hamid, come on boy."

As they walked towards Kabara once more, Haider had hope to make a stopover at a small village on the way for food and refreshments, he had saved the money for this as a contingent option. After several hours of walking in the aggressive heat, Hamid smiled in relief. Eagerly walking over towards the village, he found an uncomfortable silence of despair in the village. The tea shops and the market had been ransacked and gutted. To his horror he found a group of men stealing anything they could lay their hands on from a broken-in grocer's shop, smashing everything else they couldn't take with them.

Haider was scared for his life and Hamid's too but the poor ram was exhausted of walking for hours in the searing heat. Hamid had a slight limp to his left rear hind feet, there was no point risking injury: No one would buy an injured ram for a good price.

"Must find some shelter in these gutted buildings. My lord, for all my prayers I have made in Ahmed's name, please save me!"

With this prayer Haider lifted the ram on his shoulder and ran into one of the dark gutted buildings and hid in the basement of a gutted bookshop trembling in fear. Thirsty and exhausted, Hamid clung close to Haider digging into his chest for solace. The moments passed as limpid drops of sweat cooled on Haider's forehead until darkness fell around them and they fell asleep, safe for moment from the fear and violence that surrounded them.

011 - The long journey to the market sands — III

As the night's darkness gave way to the morning light, Haider felt relieved as there were no gunshots throughout the night nor any sudden noises to break his sleep. The ram had been resting on his owner's lap, his exhaustion worsened by dehydration. 'Must get to the market before noon, else this journey will be in vain!'
Haider got on to his feet, his ram in his arms and renewed his journey on the dusty path surrounded by the rubble of what remained of the ransacked village.

Up the mound and they had reached Kabara, Haider was happy that they made it and though one of his sandals had torn while running away from the murderous mob the other day he had some spare francs to buy a cheap pair after sending off Hamid. Though selling off Hamid would be a tough decision he would be able to buy copy books and a pen for Ahmed. The task seemed close to completion for Haider and his eyes welled up with emotion. While he was happy that he would finally put a smile to Ahmed's face if only for a few weeks: anything to get that helpless expression that would sometime cloud his little nephew's face, he would miss a familiar face in the household, that of Hamid.
'No child has to feel helpless', Haider remembered telling this to Ahmed, his only family remaining since the beginning of the civil war.

Haider's pace quickened as his optimism rose. The torn sandal left his feet but it did not bother him as he briskly walked barefeet to the market of Kabara: an open ground of blowing golden yellow sand that had pretty floral tents of merchants selling all sorts of things for the discerning buyer.

'Had pretty floral tents--', thought Haider as he was dismayed to see instead grim faced sellers sitting on the hot sands with very little to sell. Some tried to calm down their famished livestock as they grew restless with hunger in the heat.

The soul of the market had shifted from what he had felt the last time: that infectious goodwill to sell and sit happily among other sellers was missing. There seemed to be a furtiveness in the group and there was a deep charred stench in the air similar to the one when he spied upon the Daesh's killing fields.

On the far side of the market place was a smoking rubble of huts, remnants of what appeared to be an explosion. To his horror, he could make out three young boys' partially charred bodies, one of them still on fire, the other two badly bruised and bleeding from the ribs.

The stench of charred flesh overpowered Haider and he had to sit down on the hot sand with Hamid in his lap. No one in the market place spoke a word, he couldn't hear a single mother's cry for these departed sons and brothers. There was an eerie silence in the market place, most of the sellers had come to sell their animals like him.

Like Hamid, most of the cows, sheep and ram being brought here to be sold were mostly emaciated and exhausted.

'We might have to head back, how will I face my dear nephew? No, better to get back than risk losing our lives. Yet, Allah, why do I feel that I do belong here and my feet do not retrace back to my home?'

Haider's thought was accompanied by a singular vision of him looking up to the clear blue sky above with love and relief. The vision and the thought unsettled him badly as he fought to keep his composure among the remaining sellers.

Ansar Dine members appeared across the far end of the market place. They walked with purpose and all of them hide their faces with scarves which they did before delivering an enemy in Allah's name. It was a formidable sight watching them march into the market place and one could tell from their demeanour they were no ordinary civilians but dogs of war.

'Allah O Akbar! Your children burn here because the West bombed this city looking for us! Does that make you hate us? Or Kill us? Who has provided for you in these years of drought? Was it the United States of America? Was it the French, the British? NO!!! We did! We helped you when no one did! We gave you water and food when America found it easier to influence chaos with our neighbours here in Mali! Citizens of Kabara, YOU OWE US! Give yourselves to the righteous service of the Caliphate's followers!'

'We are with you, Akachi! My son still survives by your grace. Yours and the blessed Caliphate's grace will save us, accept our allegiance. Tahir, Youcef and Asad lie burning here still, please allow us to give them a proper burial!' A Family of ten, elderly and little kids fawned at the Ansar Dine leader.

'We will give them a proper burial, they are God's children, no less! However, before we do, we need to stop 'informants' from coming and leaving this village! This market needs to be cleared!

From now on, your business will be farming in your own back yards. No more assembling at the market place to buy or sell. No more music can be played in public or private, no more music instruments to be sold! All those who disobey will be punished and their musical instruments will be destroyed! We do this to protect you! Now leave and go back to your homes as we clean up this patch of sand!'

012 - The Market Massacre

An uneasy murmur rose among the sellers in the market place as all the collective gaze of the Ansar Dine and the villagers of Kabara fell on them.

'Akachi, we come here every season to sell animals, pottery and sundry goods to our wonderful customers here in Kabara! We would never think once for any harm to befall them. How else can we survive if we cannot conduct our commerce?'

As a young seller approached Akachi with this question, a faint trace of disgust passed over the latter's face. Haider surmised the Ansar Dine leader was from the western Saharan village of El Argoub. Western Saharans had a violent dislike for the people who lived along the Niger. El Argoub was a coastal village, one that could never capitalise on the promise of profitable maritime activity due to constant in fighting among the tribes. They envied the success of the enterprising and hardworking people living along the Niger and Timbuktu.

'Why has this western African come here so far from his land? What has happened to our peace loving people of Kabara?' thought Haider as he cradled the now seriously dehydrated Hamid in his lap.

'Young man, I am from El Argoub, once sworn enemies of the people of Niger! Yet, here I am today safe amongst your customers who love me and treat me as their own. Why? Because I claim to be someone who I am not?! NO!'

Akachi now faced the villagers with his back to the young man and continued:

'For years you have chosen to take the softer approach, the 'wiser' approach peddled by your moderate leaders! For years they have promised you a better society, less inter-tribe clashes, more prosperity by way of better irrigation canals!
How many of these promises have actually materialised today? You have your answer right there!
Your moderate leaders delivered little of the promises they made! And it does not matter if they meant each and every one of them!!
Look around you, your own people have become poorer by trade while these tradesmen from other tribes with their goods have become richer!!!
Does this look like equality to you? Not to me!
Inter tribe tensions are still high because now you are on the losing end of the bargain? Your moderate leaders have failed you, they have done little and that is why you chose a radical Caliphate!!!
However, fear not, for though we are swift in providing punishment and justice in the eyes of Allah! We are merciful to those who assist the Caliphate! Are you with us, citizens of Kabara?'

A raging affirmation of Akachi's question created a commotion among the sellers on the market place. This was no more a place of commerce and some of the sellers decided to leave in fear of their lives.

The villagers circled the market place refusing to allow any of the sellers to leave. The animals, upset by the commotion were pulling away from their masters with the last bit of strength in their emaciated bodies.

Haider had tears in his eyes, as his tears fell on Hamid the tired ram snuggled even tighter into Haider's chest.
'Hamid, we have to leave! Allah, what have I done? I must go back to Ahmed! He needs us, we need to be with Ahmed. Am scared, what have I done?'

Haider was holding back tears as he kept hoping that they would come out of this alive stronger, wiser. He always had: even in the most difficult times back in Timbuktu he could find ways to help Ahmed continue his studies, eat and feed his animals.

'As for you blasphemous keepers of commerce and corruption, how should we deal with you?'

Akachi motioned to his group to strap their guns on their shoulders.

This action reduced the commotion among the sellers only to break out into a stampede when all of Ansar Dine's group unsheathed their tribal daggers and went at the sellers, first pinning them to the ground and then slowly beheading them with their knives, chanting 'Allah O Akbar!' every time a severed head departed its body. Many screams were lost abruptly as their voices escaped from severed necks.
As the heads were fully severed from their bodies the body lay on the sand on its stomach with the head placed on its back. The fresh decapitation captured the last expressions of the once living

61

men: a strange resignation to their fate just before their soul left the body.

The animals broke into a stampede but were being quickly overpowered by the villager's blunt stones, sticks, knives and all form of sharp objects as they tried to break free of the blocking circle created to isolate the market massacre.

'Hamid, my dear Hamid, get up! Allah, have mercy on me! Forgive me for what I am for I have been the best Muslim I could be to my family, my brothers and strangers! Forgive me Allah!'

Hamid could no longer take the violent sight of animal and human blood spilling on the yellow market sands. The ram could be grateful for not being able to tell the overpowering sight of crimson red from the yellow sands. He kicked off Haider's lap and ran into the commotion leaving his master.

'Hamid! Hamid! My dear ram, come back! Come back, I will take care of you! Do not fear, Hamid, come back! Allah, forgive me for I only wish Ahmed's well-being. My lord, please forgive them they don't realise what they do!'

The villagers tightened the circle on the struggling sellers and their animals leaving no jugular to chance. For the first time in many, many years the market sands of Kabara turned a bright crimson red in the strangely sanguine sunset on that fateful day.

013 - Tying a plan into a timeline

Days had passed since Sam had the dossier of the Middle Eastern city in siege at his desk: he had read it through many times but dreaded his next obvious action to report it.
The besieged city was closest to the fifty billion dollar oil and natural gas reserve, the largest known source on this side of the Mediterranean.
The West, despite it's supposed 'human cost' perspective of the war had one interest that threatened to balance out its historical tyranny in the Arab Springs: Oil.

America, for all its might had a net import of oil, so did the rest of the EU. The communist behemoth had a barely sustainable net export of oil but a pipeline from the reserve right through Turkey in to land of the erstwhile Iron Curtain meant it would continue to exercise negotiable powers as the rest of the OPEC.

Kremlin felt the only way to ensure the stability of this pipeline was to give the stricken city back into the hands of the ruling despot. In return for his continued ruling capacity, the powers of the eastern bloc would look to exploiting the natural fuel reserves for several decades in exchange for diplomatic shelter as long as feasible, until American secret service could have him captured and hanged.

Drawing in his breath, Sam tried to shut out the random office noises: the whirring copier machine, the milk-frother at the coffee machine and the dull footsteps on the heavy office carpet. For a brief minute or two, what seemed like an eternity though, he felt at peace with himself. The noises faded away, it felt peaceful and he thought,

'Does death feel like this, so peaceful? God, this is just silly. Am not dead.'

'Sam, are you ok?'
It was Dave, peering incredulously through his glasses.

'For a second, I thought you were dying. Your face flushing and all.'

'Am fine. No, am ok, really. Listen we need to talk. Shall we break for lunch?'

Downstairs at the cafeteria, Sam glanced a brief look at Dave, who had an idea where their conversation would shift to.

'Look Dave, I don't know how to tell you this but it has been a year since I saw the executions on the internet a year ago. Am still processing that and now this dossier.' Sam sighed and continued, 'It's been a year since and the war has been on for five years now!'

Dave looked at Sam: he knew what his friend was going through. He had seen the executions too. This was on a website that couldn't possibly be approved by any government in the world. The internet had brought in an uncontrolled yet libertarian wave in people's lives. It wasn't legal to upload videos of violence let alone decapitation but the truth was out there like a comic streaker on a football pitch, completely starkers.

'Yet here we are in the twenty-first century and after watching such horror, no one can be the same again, right?' Dave interrupted him, then continued,

'Sam, I have seen the dossier. It has been a decade since the obvious happened: we lost the war against Kremlin, against Beijing. This war we got into was, mostly for good intentions.

Now, wait before you start! Good Intentions for the West, mostly: engaging with Kremlin on the war prevents any stability to exploit that reserve until the despot is dead. Surely that has to be good, right?'

'Collateral'

'Collateral?! When was any war without collateral? Yes, the city gets slaughtered every day but anyone out there counting whether it is an American drone or a Russian airplane dropping napalm and fire bombs? No one is counting, Sam. The locals are scurrying like rats among rubble.'

'Rats? That is just great, Dave, go on, deny yourself the guilt of this high powered perception of yourself. Four year old boy, bloody and confused, his six year old brother cannot see his brother this way knowing not what's wrong for sure but knowing his little brother is hurt and ready to leave this nightmare of a life. The younger one's hoping all this is a bad dream and he is ready to wake up in the warm arms of his mother.'

Dave fought back the helpless emotion of despair, rage and
sorrow. He realised how aligned he was to Sam's plan to
undo the grinding of the Western wheel of toxic diplomacy even
if that meant defeat of this end of the world. A defeat that could
detoxify the west of its selfish greed. Maybe the West's might
and power was only inviting more challenge to oppose it.

'Sam, we have lost this war for a decade, there is no denying our
guilt in our involvement in the Middle East but we did what we
did to keep a historical alliance stronger. There is no honour in a
lot of what we did but we are all tainted. Try not to see the
right from the wrong, it would take some effort to unravel the
two!'

'Dave, remember the dazed boy missing his lower jaw in the
video at the city hospital in eastern Aleppo? All the doctor did
was say in Arabic repeatedly taking Allah's name to forgive this
boy and take away his pain while repeatedly pointing at him like
he was a museum exhibit?'

Dave shuddered at the memory, the thought that this carnage was
more than five years in the making made him feel helpless, and
angry again.

'Internet just gave us the ability to tap into our savage
selves, Sam. In 'real-time' too.'

'We have men on the ground over in the city. We have
lost contact with them after the rebels started to use the city's
population as human shields. This dossier has a list of these
missing patriots left out there either to die. They went into the
war zone, albeit unknowingly so that we didn't have to and now
we must bring them back.'

Dave was unsettled by Sam's determination but also exhilarated by it. He remembered how on a vacation to India he would sit outside a local tea stall savouring 'chai' he had never tasted the likes of back in London. Served in little earthen pots for chump change, he would sit at the fly infested stall each morning, observing the owner's daily ritual of cleaning around his stall.

The owner would spray water around the place where he set his cart on cycle wheels. That seemed to hold the dust in place, if only for some time while he served his customers.
Then he would do this every now and then to keep the dust at bay.

Poor fella, Dave thought. Needs the garbage man to clean up to keep doing that again and again. 'Not a chance in a lifetime for the garbage man to actually clean up this mess', Dave smiled at the shopkeeper.

To Dave at this point, his choice had revealed itself in this recollection: Do we have an option but not to pay a heavy price for our past neglect and transgressions?

014 - Early Birds

It was mid-week, a slow day for most but for Eric at five am it was an early start to the day after hearing of the ceasefire between the army and the rebels. The general board meeting was called at Innofuel in the wake of the recent attacks on two of its refineries at the Golan Heights. The news condemned the attack emphasizing that the oil giant created a lot of revenue and jobs for the locals.

'Pie splitting time!' thought Eric, destined to have the board rethink the equity among the founders of the oil exploration company. From the attack on the refineries at the Golan Heights, Eric had been waiting for this moment. He had lost a dear friend in a similar mishap previously on the same site. Knowing full well that he had knowingly endangered his friend, put him at peril, the tragedy had been feeding on him, rendering him hollow from within.

'Everyone will be on board on the initial planning to start exploration within a five year plan, Eric. You don't want to be late for that one!' Joan cried out to Eric as he placed his briefcase in the car at the lobby.

Though Joan being Eric's wife had left working for the same firm years ago to raise their only son, she had never left her job at InnoFuel. Joan would read up on her previous employer's annual reports after she read Josh's bed time stories. Being an experienced accountant she preferred to get her updates on InnoFuel by looking at their annual report rather than from the news.

She knew if ever anything gave her husband a rush it was his subtle attempts to gain more influence within the board. Her job at the exploration company had given her panic attacks, bouts of 'tunnel vision'.

Being the 'softer, reasonable face' of Innofuel Explorations, every time InnoFuel with the government's support signed an MOU with a local autocratic leader in the Middle East, she would be called upon by the board to present to the world the 'facts' justifying the move.
The endless cycle of lies about exploration opening up new 'vistas of economic revival to the local population' to cover up the more direct statement of 'we are looking for the slightest opportunity to prey on your country's resources' bothered her to a point she couldn't pretend anymore. She was an accountant, not a public relations officer and just as the very public focus of being InnoFuel's spokesperson started to strain her marriage, she resigned.

Eric was the provider and whether she liked his methods or not, she would only concern herself to keep the home running. Joan did this for Josh knowing well where he would be headed if both his parents would be away dealing with the world rather than spend time with him.

'Eric, don't forget it's Josh's birthday tomorrow.'

'I wouldn't forget that, I have something planned later for tomorrow evening for the little tyke!'

'Am just saying come back on time, ok? Josh hasn't seen you around all week. He is asleep when you leave and again when you are back.'

'So you do miss me. I will make this worth the wait. What's the saying: today is the best day of the rest of your life? I will back in time, dear', Eric gave one of those rare glances which she avoided deliberately.

'Only Josh does the 'missing' you, come soon will ya?'

'I will!' Eric was already out as he slammed shut the front door, on his way to work.

Little did he realise that the board meeting at InnoFuel had taken on an older issue that he now regretted having put his hands on.

015 - Seeding the Arab Springs – I

Fifteen of InnoFuel's directors were already in the plush conference room set in its offices at the Sinclair Oil building. Eric nodded brief courtesies to them noting that the meeting had an air of urgency and purpose.
Eric decided to take this opportunity to get the ball rolling and addressed the board after briefly going through the meeting agenda fliers.

'Good morning, gentlemen. The ceasefire has happened as agreed with several of our intermediaries on the ground. What we have here is a certainty to get a team over there and restart exploration based on the country's disavowed geo surveyors? Come on now, cards on the table please! Brian? '

Eric had noted Brian's detachment from the proceedings and prodded him to break his reverie. Brian was one of the oldest directors of InnoFuel from among the rest. Being one of the longest serving directors of the company, his face had the trademark withered, tired look that his colleagues and friends had come to identify with. He was the alpha male in this pack, but an aging, disconcerted and desolate one at that.

'Guys, just to set the scene here, how many of us have built a career living off the instabilities in the Middle East? Most of us, yes. We started back in the Fifties when we invaded the Suez Canal by the orders of 'yours truly' President Eisenhower and showed the French and the British the door. We understandably support Israel for obvious reasons but our alliance meant consuming the rest of the Arab world save for Riyadh's royal kingdom!'

'Brian, that kept us supplied for ages: the Oil prices were kept in control, no other Arab nation can barely come out of their senses having faced unreliable dictators and rebels supported by the U.S. just long enough to keep the arms deals going. Instability in the Middle East is what keeps our homes warm in the winter and feeds us. Is old age bringing out the idealist in you or are you just ready to retire?'

Eric's words echoed in the stunned silence as he lounged back on his chair, staring into Brian's deep set eyes.

'Eric, you will have your say once am finished and I will make it quick: About two decades ago, and this did not have much to do with oil as much as it had to do with opium, though there was the possibility of natural gas exploration in Afganistan. The U.S Army armed the local rebels fighting the communist forces with all the ammunition that any US army would require to decimate the communists. You do remember this was the 'Taliban' as we knew it at the time?

Once Russia left the subcontinent, our interest in the region promptly turned to the 200 billion dollar opium industry used to make grade 'A' heroin. We left without closing in on our assistance to the destroyed country, destroyed largely by our own selfish and largely destructive motives. Few decades later, the Taliban, whom we had armed to fight the war turned back on us, attacking American sovereignty in the exact same manner as we did theirs. Bin Laden was public enemy in the eyes of the American, but how many Americans actually ponder over the fact that we brought this war to our home because we did bad business, unethical business over arms, drugs and natural resources? For our country this goes hand in glove: the oil supplies the 'probable cause' and the arms supply the means to keep political status quo the way we want to keep selling our ammo and a sweet deal on the oil!'

'Thanks for the moral speech, Brian, but where are we getting to with this? We are businessmen not murderers, for God's sake. Damascus presents an opportunity that, correct me if am wrong, the West seems to be willing to lose! Now, in the face of this apparent 'defeat', what do we do? We are a unilateral exploration company. Yes, we have been privy to many of the defence's secrets about their ground preparations before but that information is not public, right? Is there a way we can get our men in Damascus to start carting off that 50 billion dollar reserve sitting there? The Rumeilan region needs help, we can provide that but I guess the question is how?'

Arthur was worried for his friend, both of them had joined InnoFuel about the same time 40 years back and it meant a great deal to have Brian's approval on their plans for today.

'Arthur, you are missing the point. Anyway back to Bin Laden, the leader of the rebel group decides to land two airplanes on the WTC. I guess now the question is: yes, it was a tragedy but is this personal collateral to any of you? For me it was, I lost my only daughter and grandson to the North Tower collapse. What has it been like, nearly two decades? All these years I have been doing my job, raging with grief while the president hounded that bastard and not until Laden got killed did I realise that the avenged killing didn't set anything right. Laden wasn't the devil as the government led people to believe, it was us. All hatred for

Laden left me and I felt nothing but regret, regret at we have been doing and are about to continue doing.

We haven't learnt from our little misadventure with Saddam either and we are marching the exact same beat here with the Syrian people, except that we have lost this time to the commies. Good for us and good for the world! The point being, leave this to the Russians, we should only get on the ground if they let us or we take a step back.'

Eric could not deny Brian's point, but he couldn't back out of what he had planned for today, earlier this morning:
'Brian, the commies will never let us through you know that. Hell, they have even decimated the rebels off most of their major cities, our help notwithstanding. Let me push this to the White House through an intermediary, see how they can help us? Who in the board are with me on this?'

All the director's nodded their heads in approval except for Brian and Arthur.

'Arthur?'

'I need Brian on board on this, Eric. Brian has been here the longest, his knowledge is invaluable to the negotiations at all levels. Brian, help me out here, buddy?'

016 - Seeding the Arab Springs — II

Eric was happy with the outcome of the meeting: Arthur had managed to convince Brian to approve the plan. The board of directors needed a new executioner of plans and Eric was called to the task.

Driving back home in his range-rover, Eric had a cigarette on his right hand and his left on the wheel. Blowing the smoke out the window he could not suppress the smile curling up his lips: it was perfect. He was InnoFuel's sole representative to the government of the United States with a window view to the classified destabilisation plans, a bullet proof access to Damascus.

His 'later hours' meeting with the White House intermediary, a pro-Israel lobbyist gave a broad outline of what the federal government were about to do as they did in Arab Springs back in 2011:

a) Supplant the losing rebels for the time being with well-educated middle class Syrians to instigate violence against the current regime, claiming at atrocities by the government during the ceasefire.

b) Have the drones' bomb the evacuation buses en-route between the besieged cities using non traceable napalm and chemical firebombs which would leave no trace of any chemical warfare. Yet the symptoms of chemical warfare would be visible on the victims which would place the blame squarely on the current regime.

Eric paused at this thought though: children would be involved, families would get hurt no doubt. Real people in need of help stretching out their hands, in need of help. Only to be chopped off at the knees, poor bastards.

'Fucking Arab turds never learn, do they? Look at what they did to a helping hand in Europe, bastards. They deserve much more.' Eric justified the terrible thought treating the end result, his ultimate goal as a means to gain more power in InnoFuel, as a 'by product' of his actions.

And finally c) During ceasefire, get the rebels trapped in Al-Raqqah out of the region before the UN Tribunal found out their true identity, this would essentially be a search and rescue, or a search and terminate mission in case things went south.

At the back of his mind, he did wonder whether the attack in Berlin was a planned attack to instigate the far right in Europe. The attack on a country who have been the source of oppression during the world wars opens its gates as a humanitarian move to allow those who have fled oppression. Only to be attacked by the same people that left the populace rooting for the right wing. It sounded too predictable to be true but Eric let this thought slip: he had no intention but to make tidy profit in terms of power in this plan.

Unable to believe his luck at getting this far so easily, Eric contemplated the thought that all of today might have been a bit too easy: how did it all go so smoothly? In all of ten years at InnoFuel he never had it so good, yet now the wheels seemed well oiled in motion. No hang-ups, perfect plan for an initial non-violent instigation against the commies and the dictator.

It was Plan B that he was worried about: considering all else failed the only option would be a full blown invasion of Syria and a 'gaddafi style' execution of the dictator on grounds on inhuman 'massacre' and 'genocide' of a nation's people.
This could effectively turn the war completely in favour of the communist bloc with full blown veto on the UN Security Council and this time, with the retreat of British and French military support, any hopes of entering the naturally resourceful land of the Arabs will be lost forever.

Eric pondered all of this while driving back home and casually glanced at his watch: he hadn't realised that he was very late for Josh's birthday, it was 9pm. He drove faster to cover the remaining miles to get to his son's birthday party in time. He was late, again.

017 – Present cause, Lost Family – I

'Why did you join us, Naim? Are you avenging family or friends or is it the glory of the jihad you seek? Five years fighting together and every time I ask, you turn to stone. You have to tell me before I loan your boots to someone else when the time comes?'

Ahmed looked at me with a questioning face of a chemistry teacher. Ah, the light moments of my days when Ahmed would be in a mood such as this. He asked this several times in the last few years but I was too driven by rage and desolation to answer him with any more except a look in the distance at the dusty horizon with only one question in my mind: were they still alive?

'Tie my boots to my dead feet right to grave, Ahmed. Mahmud's love will stay on my heels till I die, God bless him! I did start to fight for our cause as I have a wife and boy taken hostage and rumour has it that they were last seen in A'zaz. I do this to get closer every day to the possibility of meeting them. For Omar and Sara, Ahmed! I wouldn't be able to rest until I see them once again.

For Mahmud who never for once mentions that fateful day when our world came crashing down at Qatmah and for you, my dimpled brother, whose genuine pain and sacrifice I have seen among the greed and the blood lust of most other rebels!'

You will meet them, Ahmed, when you will take little Omar in your arms and Sara who will no doubt honour you as my brother!'

'Your son will love me more than he would love you, Naim! After all who is the softer, funnier and lovable one among us? He will have my intellect, brains and charm, I will school him to be the great scholar that I never could be. He will be worthy of the Ahmad Baba library scholarship in my time, my little niece!'

'As long as you don't fill his head with the anti-west nonsense we are going to be just fine. My boy is five now, Ahmed and I just celebrated his birthday with a small prayer last night.'

'Five? He is five years old? Naim, do you mean you last saw him as a new born? Isn't that hoping too much? We have fought all these battles and we have seen what happens to abandoned children. I admire your hope and courage but look around us, haven't you seen enough? This is a dream for the fool's paradise! How do we know that they are alive and well?'

In my heart I was never convinced that they had died. At the time and this was five years back, our village, Qatmah, was surrounded by the army forces after we had started a ritual of burning rogue rebels from the Caliphate who had defected to the army. The stories of our punishment of the rebels and the acrid smoke of frequently burning human flesh had brought them to the village.

My wife, baby in her arms was cowering in the thatched roof house where we lived amid the hostile cries and shouts outside in the village grounds. Sounds of terrified cows and sheep running to save themselves permeated the senses in between bursts of rapid fire guns. The army were rounding up the village members as they got hold of them.

My mind at times plays tricks on me in regards to my exact retelling of the events. It was traumatic enough to experience, let alone retell.

An image of my wife breast-feeding our baby son Omar would be fleeting cross my mind. The next image would be of her cowering in fear within the hut as I go outside to check on the commotion at the market sands.

The final image is of the stars as I lay on my back, defeated and desolate as I see a beautiful little girl's feet protrude out, pale and defiant against the fire consuming her flesh and that of other villagers.

This was the first time in my life I could truly understand the acute feeling of loss and its true definition: my wife and my baby boy were no more with me.

That was five years ago, A'zaz was forsaken by the Caliphate who forbade us to go there and meet our families. The land belonged to the Northern Storm now.

Ahmed's concerned gaze upon me jolted me right back to my situation where I was, sitting empty handed with nothing but a dream. I was miles away from them with ill laid plans to rescue with them, I still had a long way to go.

'I shouldn't hope but I have to know, Ahmed. God knows I have been trying and I will go to A'zaz with hope now that the ceasefire will force the Caliphate to look elsewhere to spread their influence.'

'You will be called a deserter and beheaded for it, Naim!'

'Omar is your nephew, Ahmed. He is the closest we can get to see a hopeful future ahead of us, without war and suffering one day. What would you not do to have that one shot in life to shelter a rose in this desert?'

'Naim, it is dangerous to speak of hope, love and a future in this place, such intentions are trampled with far more ferocity than those who met the enemy eye to eye. Inshallah, may the lord deliver you to them although either extreme joy or extreme sorrow awaits you on that horizon which I fear might change you for good or for worse.
My own nephews and nieces had slipped out into the city and never came back. Such crevices this city has that can claim the innocent without a trace!'

'They are alive else why am I breathing still? I must meet them, Ahmed or at least try to find out what happened to my family but will you help me when the time comes?'

'Ahmed has never left watching your back what makes you think I will quit now? Naim, can I ask you why Mahmud treats you as his own son? I see in his eyes the fatherly love for you as my uncle Haider had for me. Why does Mahmud love you so much more than me, after all that I have done for him? I am his relative after all, yet he loves you more than I. The men say he changed after the tragic events at Qatmah but they refuse to say further. What happened to him at Qatmah before I came here?'

'Spare Mahmud this question if you truly love him, Ahmed. Both of us lost our family at Qatmah. I couldn't tell you much either except the wound is too deep and it runs through Mahmud and I. He knows one day I will set my pace on this quest, he fears losing his only son so he will try to stop me only to finally let me go.'

At the time the call for prayers came and we sat down for prayer.

'You will join me, won't you Ahmed? I feel overwhelmed taking onto this search all by my own. I couldn't bear losing them again.'

'Say no more, Naim. From one brother of Islam to another, I will join you to help you find your family. Even more so as a friend; now let us pray.'

My heart was buoyed by Ahmed's reply but sank a little when he mentioned the 'arab' brotherhood. To me it was a betrayal of our friendship to not have divulged my true self to him: I am his brother but not from this land but a nation several seas across, one that he probably viewed with suspicion. I will tell him one day when we wouldn't have to worry about these irrelevant details. We prepared for the evening prayer as the calls for prayers were sounded.

'May Allah give Naim his family who will always be in my prayers besides Uncle Haider!'

Ahmed's honest prayer made my longing for my family more severe as I felt Omar and Sara in close proximity as we prayed together.

018 – Present cause, Lost Family – II

'I can't come with you, Naim, I can't. The Ansar Dine have promised me to help me find out about my uncle Haider, back in Qabara. Akachi, the famed Daesh leader himself has promised me having heard my plight from the elders. I have only but his blessing and his support to find my only family, Naim!'

For the first time in my life, I had a sinking feeling in my stomach. My only friend left in this world would have to part ways now for the exact same reasons I had to part ways with the Caliphate. I could probably manage most of the rough terrain and the odd skirmish by myself but the thought of parting with Ahmed made me weaker.

'I will help you, Naim. Let us first go to the elders, give them this ordnance map that they have been after then we plan your escape, okay friend?

We had crossed over from down the hills, literally crawling on our bellies as we made our way back across the village grounds into the flat roofed decrepit building where the elders were waiting with the Caliphate's most loyal sect, the Ansar Dine's elite troops waiting in the back.

As we crossed across the front door, we were greeted with cries of the lord from some of the waiting foot soldiers. One of them came up to me with his mother and what appeared to be Youcef's sister, her face so similar to the young man killed in the ambush.

'Youcef? Where is he?'

I shook my head, hesitantly and moved on with Ahmed before the tears of the mother and her family could overwhelm me. God rest that boy's soul, it was not his time to die.

'Ahmed, my loyal soldier, come over here! Naim, my ever reliable lieutenant, meet Akachi our new leader from the Caliphate, just transferred from the African sands after years of helping the Tuaregs rediscover the righteous path of the prophet Mohamed!'. It was Mahmud Nasser, our elder and reporting field leader introducing the tall African to us.

'Salaam Aleikum, commander. Were you there in the Tuareg rebellion a few years ago?'

Ahmed's eyes lit up approvingly at Akachi, who was obviously taking a liking for his latest fan.

'Yes, indeed. We cleaned up the scour of cockroaches in that land, my friend. We cleansed it and it required a lot of blood, mind you!'

The elder, Mahmud Nasser, was not trained in combat but considered by many as the one who held sway in our village. People loved to listen to him in the evening if he ever made a public appearance to cheer up the people. Rumour had it that

Mahmud had kept a secret library full of the nation's lost treasures such as guides, historical scriptures, maps, books and other invaluable trinkets.

He himself had admitted that he saved this for once the war was over, it is the knowledge of these treasures that would rebuild this once great nation. For this the right time and the right person was key and he would not share it unless he knew when the time was right to share those secrets. Right now, he was quite keen on the map.

'Where is the map, Naim? It is the treasure of our village, I know it. Give it to me, I know the perfect place to store it for our grand children!'

'Not so fast, Mahmud! We had an agreement on this particular map, remember?'

Akachi was sharp and incisive in reminding Mahmud of his negotiated agreement: the map for the protection of his village from the armed forces.

I handed the map to Akachi and a thought crossed my mind of Akachi being quite ruthless and being a danger to the very existence of this village.

Ahmed glanced at me, then back at Akachi: the thought that Akachi would be selling the map directly to the communist regime was surpassed by the one question that was dear to his hear at this point: Could Akachi tell him about Uncle Haider?

'I believe our loyal lieutenant Ahmed has some request to make of you, Akachi! I will leave you to it.'

Mahmud motioned towards Ahmed and went off to meet his other soldiers, offering tea to the tired ones himself.

I thought, looking at him and the one thought that stayed in my mind: Florence of Crimea. He was doing exactly the same service in this war. May God bless him and keep him alive.

'Akachi, my uncle Haider and I used to live in Timbuktu, near Sankore Madrassah. Do you know the madrassah there, sir?'

'Sankore Madrassah? Yes, I was there in the Tuareg rebellions in 2012. Were you there then? How did you manage to come here, lieutenant?'

'Akachi, my uncle Haider had gone to the market sands to sell our last ram, Hamid. We had little food and no money. I was still trying to complete my education at the time at the Sankhore Madrassah---'

'You were a scholar at the madrassah? Which degree, son?'

'The superior degree, sir! I had the patronage of Sheikh Nasser, one of the most demanding Islamic teachers in the madrassah.'

'And the most famous too! Son, haven't you heard? The sheikh has died, publicly beheaded at the outskirts of Timbuktu during the Tuareg rebellion?'

019 – Present cause, Lost Family – III

'Allah, forgive us! Why? Why was he beheaded, Syed Akachi? What had he done? What was his crime?'

Akachi's face hardened, remembering back those years when he was judge, jury and executioner for the Caliphate.

'Sheikh Nasser was a traitor, he had been passing invaluable intelligence to the army and the communist forces, giving up secrets of our activities to our invaders! Some said he had become a recluse over time and spent less time being the spiritual leader at the madrassah.
He would spend more time at his library until one day he just went about talking to people wildly about some 'persistent western propaganda' that was more poisonous than our government, our dictator and the communist forces! Mad fool kept trying to talk to people in the city centre until one of the onlookers informed us and we came to visit him.'

Akachi's memory of the short bloody visit sent a slight panic down his spine but his experienced, ruthless demeanour suppressed the feeling. His mind wandered to that fateful day in

Timbuktu but was careful not to divulge beyond what was meant to be revealed to Ahmed.

'Akachi! How dare you disrespect me, the great sheikh Nasser of Sankhore madrassah, of true blooded lineage?! You drag me here to the city center and ask me to explain my comments to the people of my village?

These people have a right to know, the Arab Springs were never raised by the people on their own. Yes, the Arab Springs have nothing to do with the people here but it is where the seeds of conflict were sown!

The Arab Springs were seeded by the capitalist western powers whose only interest in the region is oil! Initially they tried to instigate non-violent strife to destabilise regimes with whom they had no favour. Once that did not work, their intelligence agencies started arming the rebels with lethal weapons capable of starting a war and that is how it all began!'

Akachi felt cold to the bone: what if the villagers who were listening on believed the sheikh? He knew that this was not supposed to be common knowledge, especially among the poor and uneducated in this country. What Sheikh Nasser implied was a problem to the Ansar Dine and Daesh's survival in this region. He still tried to reason with the sheikh.

'Sheikh Nasser! Are you trying to say that the Ansar Dine or the Daesh are puppets of the West? This is blasphemy! You call the soldier of Allah an unrighteous puppet at the hands of others?!

Listen to this, you village folks! The sheikh has lost his head, he has stopped teaching the wisdom of Allah at the monastery and clearly the books and the West have pickled his brain! Maybe the sheikh has enough support from the government to make this claim! OR maybe, he is just gone mad like a frothing rabid dog!

Listen, you all, who protected you and fired back at the army forces making them retreat? Us!
Who helped you get food during the drought? Where was the government then? Who helped you?'

'Ansar Dine!' roared the crowd back in unison.

'Down with the sheikh! Down with the traitor and Allah's enemy!'

At this Akachi ripped off the sheikh's turban and threw it to the crowds. His accompanying soldiers tied the sheikh's hands and took him towards the 'traitor's' pit just outside of the village.

Akachi started recording a video of the beleaguered sheik being pushed down to the pit. The sheikh was shivering, his head exposed his white robe dragging along in the sands, walking unevenly barefooted on the sands.

Being brought to the pit, the sheikh started saying prayers asking Allah to forgive his executioners of this heinous crime and cleanse them of many more crimes they had committed.

Akachi pushed his neck to the ground and said these final words to the sheikh.

'Seems like I do not have to execute you, Nasser! You blabber prayers for our redemption whereas it is you who needs it, you infidel dog, son of Satan! Who has a blunt knife? Seems the sheikh has lost his head, let's make it count!'

'You are the traitor, Akachi! You are just a mercenary in the hands of the West! Your time will come, Inshallah!'

The last words of the noble sheikh, now he prayed for a quick end.

'Allah o Akbar!' chanted the group as one of Akachi's soldiers started to dismember Nasser's head from his body with a blunt knife. Precious blood rolled down the pit. Nasser being a wealthy sheikh was quite healthy and had a thick neck, initially the terror showed in his eyes but slowly lost their life after the knife went under his throat.
It was not a quick execution on account of the blunt knife ,took forever until the head came free of his body while the soldier tried to sever the head from the top and then again from the softest part of the neck.
Once it did, everyone chanted 'Allah o Akbar! Victories to Allah's soldiers!' and the soldier placed the head on the dead sheiks back, the white tunic absorbing his blood.

Akachi stopped recording, it was enough to have him promoted and out of this country into the heartland of the conflict: Syria. A Promotion. New lands to conquer. A 'worthy' transfer to the Middle East.

020 – Present cause, Lost Family – IV

'What did finally happen to Sheikh Nasser, Syed Akachi?'

Ahmed's question was earnest: he loved and respected Sheikh Nasser but had learnt to be an impartial man of principles from the sheikh himself when he was still a disciple.

'No, he could not be reasoned with, son. In the end, the villagers asked for the traitor to be executed and he was executed.'

Ahmed was moved by the blunt words of the commander, for a while he forgot to ask about Haider.

'Let us talk more tomorrow, soldier. We have a mission to re-take the eastern side of the city, you and your friend will join me tomorrow on this noble cause. Let us rest now, soldier. Allah Hafiz!'

As Akachi left for his night's rest, Ahmed beckoned him to wait.

'Commander Sir, I bade you a restful sleep before tomorrow's mission. I almost forgot of my uncle, Haider. He had left from Timbuktu during the hot month of May, 2012. It was the second week if I remember. He went to Kabara to sell his ram for money and food for me. Do you know any news of Kabara? I hear none, Sir, the village elders forbade us to go there saying that the residents of Kabara did not wish to do business with us. Is that true, commander? Why did the residents of Kabara close their doors to us?'

Akachi's face was frozen and grave, I noticed a faint trace of fear on his face which changed to exasperation, finally back to indifference. There was more to this man that what was told of him, of what we knew of him.

'Soldier, I have told you enough. About Kabara, the villagers no more trusted the people of Timbuktu. All your people did was to bring unnecessary expensive items to them to corrupt their women and children! Your people brought this disrepute among them by their foul business practices! Now it is time for rest soldier and I bade you rest as well. You will need it tomorrow, Ahmed!'

Ahmed was hurt but his question was left unanswered by the commander: what had happened to his dear uncle Haider?

As it emerged, Mahmud had planned an incursion into the eastern end of Aleppo, this time we would be accompanied by a new group joining the fray: the Kurdish YPG would formally join us, the Free Syria Army.

'This war has run long enough and we need all the help we can get. Don't be bothered by the Kurds: tomorrow, your group will be five in all, equal participation from each group with an impartial leader in Akachi. Allah be always with you, Ahmed and Naim, you have been like sons to me'

Mahmud kissed our foreheads and left, I thought I saw tears in his eyes. Mahmud had been like a father to both of us, he has always seen us coming back more often than others these last few years. My heart bade him a fond goodbye knowing well that I may never return here tomorrow. One knot remained. Ahmed.

'Ahmed, this will be my last mission, friend, come with me. I don't ask because I need help from you but because I will be without a friend!'

Ahmed was already in a whirlwind of emotions after hearing of Nasser. Pushing me away, shrugging he looked away.

'The great Akachi accused my master of treachery! I know my master, he was as gentle and soft as a rose petal, as straight as the desert cacti thorn!'

'Ahmed, I do not trust Akachi. Even worse, we are to be led by him and with two Kurds who have no interest in this country's wellbeing. I saw a shadow of doubt in his eyes when he spoke of Nasser and your uncle. He is lying, I can tell!'

'Shall we return alive tomorrow? Allah, show me the truth, show me the way!'

Before I could comfort my dear friend it was time for our prayers. We knelt together, as we prayed I felt God touch my heart for yet probably another time. And I felt for my brother, a brother I never had before, my friend.

May he find truth, may God shield him from the need to avenge and give justice for his family without rage, anger and malice. Inshallah.

021 – Crossroads

As I donned my fatigues with rifle rounds for our mission, the Kurds were preparing theirs and with a slight sense of unease I realised that their ammo was an upgrade from our own.
With dismay, I realised that the ammo was early 2010 American army issue. The upgrade from our own meant the 'brotherhood' were in on this mission for their own agenda, not ours.
Ahmed had followed my gaze and he nodded to me, beckoning me to finish counting my provisions. He hadn't slept all night I could tell judging by his tired eyes, the question of his uncle eating away from inside knowing that one man had the answers to all his questions. Akachi would be leading us today in an attempt to reclaim parts of the lost city.

'Are we ready, team? Ahmed and Naim, cover our entrance from the rear end of truck as we make our way to the eastern edge of the city. As for you two Kurds, look sharp for snipers at the front. Miss them once and they will certainly not miss you! I will take the heavier sub-machine in the middle helping you out. Allah O Akbar! Allah O Akbar!'

As the group cheered on in unison, we made our way over what remained of the road reduced into a rubble track. I looked over at Mahmud who smiled at us from the group with those kind eyes that we had come to trust in this world stripped of any such emotion. I waved back at him and raised my rifle to salute him.

Turning back to Ahmed, I felt Akachi's stare upon my friend with the look of a lion about to pounce on his prey.
An hour into our journey and much as I had started to hate Akachi, I was afraid of him. He seemed every inch the butcher I thought he was. Though we were on a way to a mission and fear had left my mind, my hands never left my rifle as our truck lumbered over the bumpy roads.

'You two, good friends? I have seen you two pray together!'

'Do you have any friends, Akachi? Or all they all dead?' I asked this seemingly ruthless man as I tried to connect the dots between his positions as an Ansar Dine leader to his current position of top Daesh operative. Those ruthless eyes seemed to hold secrets which I wouldn't want to know, yet it seemed he was more aware of the plight of Ahmed's family than he would care to share.
The dark African started smiling in sarcasm and while I expected a menacing repartee I held my gun tightly, safety unlocked.

'Zzzt! Zzzt!' The unmistakeable whispers of silenced bullets grazed our truck. At first I thought they were sounds from a bee though my instinct told me to duck. Sniper Shots!

'Ahmed! Down!' I shouted as Akachi swung the gun towards the direction of the bullets and fired away as the truck swerved to a narrow alley in the city.

'взять их(Take them)! взять их!' shouted one in Russian from the third storey of a dilapidated hospital.Almost within moments ten Russian soldiers formed a perfect defence formation, they were waiting for us. To my horror and disbelief, one of them picked up what appeared to be an RPG launcher.

'RPG! RPG! take the truck into the underground parking lot of the hotel ahead! Ahmed ---'

Before I could finish, we heard the RPG launch, all of us jumped off the truck , except for the driver who had no time to react. The truck exploded behind our backs taking down the hapless driver with it.
Falling hard on the rubble, five of us ran into the darkness of the underground parking, desperately running up the stairs to the top floor rooms to create vantage points for our defense.

'Get your sniper rifles, you two! Guard the staircase , see if they pursue us!' Akachi snarled at us and took the two Kurds to the roof with him while we guarded the door at the roof.

The Russians did not follow us into the staircase as they had succeeded in disabling our ride out into the city. It was a matter of time before their foot soldiers found us now that we were marked and cornered carrying guns without silencers. Though we had the higher ground, Akachi and his Kurdish foot soldiers made the most of it firing at the soldiers barricaded behind the hospital windows. Much to my dismay, their rifle mags were smoking due to the continuous shooting: without taking a break they were running the risk of jamming them as they got hot.

'Damned Kurds will bring the whole army down upon us! Ask them to stop firing--'

'Allah O Akbar!', the war cry was all too familiar but coming off Akachi it sounded like a curse.Oddly enough I felt eyes on me and turned to find Akachi cocking his rifle to fire at Ahmed. For the first time ever, I fired at one within my own group. Akachi dropped his rifle, palm shredded by bullets off my M16 rifle.

Ahmed was on him as well as the Kurds looked on , first at Akachi then at themselves,unsure what to do.

'Akachi, you filthy traitor! Somebody put this man out of his misery! Sheikh Nasser was not a traitor if you wouldn't pull a gun at me!'

'Go on, Ahmed! Sully your hands with my blood! How fateful I felt when I came to know both of those whom you loved were slaughtered by my own hands!'

Ahmed realised the reason for Akachi's hawk eyed stare while they began their mission. He realised that Akachi had felt powerful in the knowledge that he had known an entire chain of men who knew, loved and respected each other, that he would effectively cleanse this link of love and hope with the end of Ahmed's life at his hands. Such a thought gave great power to this proud, dangerous vile vanguard of the Ansar Dine.

'Don't listen to him, Ahmed! Give him justice, not vengeance, my friend. Execute him but with a prayer forgiving him. Remember the words, the teachings we believe in!'

I could no longer recognise Ahmed, his face had nothing but vengeance and anger, relishing at the thought of cruelty he would inflict upon Akachi. Unsheathed his dagger he proceeded to carve Akachi's face.

At this the Kurds raised their guns and were about to train them on my friend, I shot both of them. They fell with exit wounds off their spleen, one of them still alive.

'How do I contact the 'brotherhood'? You have no business being so far into this country!' I shouted my question to the one alive.

The living one weakly said 'Traitor! You will never find the 'brotherhood' by yourself! Wait, are you American?!'

The last words of the Kurd were heard by Ahmed as a cry of pain left his victim. By now he had made Akachi's face unrecognisable with his unsheathed dagger but the vanguard was alive still.

Ahmed turned to me, 'Naim? You are not shia? are you western infidel? you... you are not muslim? My friend, whom I thought more as my brother? Did he say the truth? Why would he lie, Naim? Why would a dying man lie?!'

'Ahmed, whoever I may be, called by a different name, I am and always will be your friend! what other people know of me , or I know them will never ever change our bond,brother. I only survive to find my wife and son. A hundred lives we have had, miraculous escapes, all that hopefully lead us to the truth! I had to keep this secret even from myself to survive!

Ahmed was desolate, overcome with grief.Hopelessness and anger were pushing, nudging the Ahmed I knew out of his body, out of his soul.And then the bleeding devil spoke one last time.

'In my pocket is a mobile phone I cut off a priest's hand in

Timbuktu. I was something of a cameraman, you see. Had my undertaken executions recorded, you might find your uncle in there hanging off a tree, maybe. Or smouldering under burnt tyres. It's all there, take it!'

This man had no fear, he was certain Ahmed would execute him but till his last breath, the devil provoked Ahmed to bring out the worst in him.

'Go, Naim. Leave now. Remember you don't leave as a friend of mine! My family and my friends are all dead! Leave for your family. I will stay here, I have much work left to do on my friend here while he is still alive. Go!'

Ahmed's rejection of our friendship broke me from within. It felt a glorious beam of light was eclipsed by something that blocked it completely. I had to leave and did so without saying a word. Turning around, I thought I would never see my friend again.

When I did, he was searching frantically in Akachi's phone of any traces of his uncle Haider. Our friends and family never leave us, not even after death. We still keep looking for them in life, and beyond.

022 - Onward to A'zaz - I

A'zaz was little more than a day's journey by foot from the hotel where we had the skirmish with the Russian snipers on the ground. The air was still thick with the burnt stench of spent ammunition as I attempted to rationalise the journey I was about to make.

'What were the Russians doing on the ground? They had been content on aiding the army from the air in this part of the city!' The thought bothered me even more as I turned around to look back at the hotel from where I emerged. My heart pounding, a terrible guilt engulfed me in sorrow as I made out Ahmed's silhouette up in the hotel windows finishing off Akachi, the latter's screams echoed through the broken hotel windows. My heart was heavy, I had betrayed Ahmed's trust and left him desolate and hopeless. He had adopted me as a brother, protected me from those stray bullets when I had given up. I had left him alone at a time when he needed me the most.

'God forgive me for I have not been the brother Ahmed has been to me. Ahmed, I hope to meet you again asking for your forgiveness!'
I prayed hoping that this abrupt parting with my friend would not make my rescue plans for Sara and Omar count against my decision.

I would not risk borrowing a vehicle for any part of my journey through these sniper infested streets. The safest path would be through the dark of the night weaving through the buildings, avoiding the main streets. I slipped away from one building to another, stopping every time I thought I heard a footstep in the gravel or a movement on the dirt and rubble of the destroyed city around me.

Around a dark corner of the moonlit roads I saw a woman and child standing afar. The boy, about five years old was holding on to his mother's hand and they appeared to be nothing but an apparition in this desolate night. They reminded of Sara and Omar who had become apparitions in my memory themselves. Five years had passed trying to get through the border and yet no news of them: were they alive and would this be a futile attempt to rescue them?

'Sara, are you still in A'zaz? Did you make your way to the mosque at Kilis for your refuge? Is Omar all right after all that travel through the desert?'

Tears welled up in my eyes as I remembered how complicit I had made Sara in my decision to accept a position as the geo-scientist lead for InnoFuel at their new exploration setup on the Golan Heights.

My tranquil life during my work on the oil scarce Black Sea oil rig seemed a faraway dream. Every Friday as I took the flight to London I looked forward to those weekends with my dear wife, it would be a perfect end to a tough week. Sara was a tough practical woman on the inside and though difficult to reason with at times yet she loved Len far too much to be making decisions with her head.

My longing grew for someone who never left me as my shadow, yet I had no idea what to expect in A'zaz after vain attempts to reach the town in all these years.

One life changing event converted me from Len to Naim, for the sake of our safety. I was Len, son of immigrant Israeli parents, naturalised citizens of Great Britain, schooled in North London. Len seems so far away from myself now: carefree, happy but a hasty decision maker with everything going for him in life. Len was more content than Naim, happily married to Sara, looking forward to a settled desk job for Innofuel closer to London after all the challenging explorations he had undertaken at the behest of his mentor and friend, Eric.

Life was about to change when Innofuel's blue blood called upon him for a meeting at the Sinclair Oil building in Manhattan. Len had just come back to their London home after the long flight back from New York. He felt tired and jaded after the meeting with Eric and had taken a flight straight back after. Though Eric was his friend and mentor for many years, the meeting had its moments in creating a few rough edges as the assignment was a hard-sell to Len. Not wishing to stay in the city in whose shadows sharks seemed to lurk he headed straight for home, feeling his worries slip away seeing Sara busy in their kitchen at home.

'Sara, there is a slight change in plans. Sara, are you listening? This is important.'

Sara was making dinner for us, despite having a hard day at work she would always make dinner than order takeout. Her love was always omnipresent in my life in such subtle ways.

'Eric has left me with no choice but to take up a temporary position as chief consultant at the Golan Heights. I have to leave for three months and I had him promise me a desk job at the London office later though, but it is going to be a little while longer to get there, ok?'

'Three Months?' Putting her finger on the globe on my desk, 'Isn't that the middle east? Golan Heights is disputed land for decades! Eric has no business sending you there. You didn't say yes, did you? You did?! When were you going to tell me?'

'I will be back in three months, you won't even know I wasn't here, Sara. We can put all this travelling behind us for good after this assignment. Eric chose me because there is no fear of a lack of safety and security anymore. The area is well protected by the UN too! He knows he needs a consultant who understands the local workforce better than anyone else. He said 'I can speak and play the part being a Jew!''

'You aren't going alone, Mr. Berkowicz! Am not going to mope around in London for three months, waiting for you.'
Sara rested her back against the wall. As much as she hated Len making decisions that affected both of them, she loved him.

'Sara, there are as many ways to get to jail over there without a good reason as there are many ways to say 'hi'. Stay here and I will be so much more relieved that you are safe here in London!'

'Am not convinced of Eric's reassurances around the safety over there, Len. 'No news is good news' was usually true when we were younger, in this day and age falling below the attention radar is the next worse event to dying itself. No, am not leaving you alone with some queer eyeing your butt. Seriously, Len, I cannot bear not having to see you for weeks let alone months. Don't argue with me on this!'

'Queers eyeing my---no, I didn't hear that, did I? I didn't want you to say it but I was hoping you would. This could mean you have to take a really long break from your job, are you up to that?'

Even in the most difficult differences of opinion we never lost respect in each other. We kissed, Sara hugged me for a long time. For a while, we just kept that moment of us being in our London apartment in our hearts like a snapshot.

The next week we landed on the Fik Airfield where a truck convoy took us to the exploration's worker colony at the Golan Heights.

Our spirits were buoyed by the beautiful approach to the Heights, however, the convoy veered off the road onto a vast barren wasteland. There was an uneasy calm and looking into the distance I realised why: to the west beyond a water tower were the Al Nusra stations and beyond that a tank of the Syrian Army were clearly visible.

'Am glad you are here, Sara but I didn't want you to see the situation on the ground. I wasn't expecting this military presence all around the plot!'

I motioned her to look at the group of rebels from the Al Nusra Islamist Group discussing with the army personnel in our trucks on the road ahead. One of them mentioned 'I.E.D.' on the road ahead in Arabic.

'There is a Syrian planted I.E.D. in the road ahead, we will need to go off road, sir'

The truck driver spoke to me in Arabic, turning around and taking a road over a barren stretch. The pact between the army and the Al Nusra looked incredibly weak and one sided. Neither Sara nor I felt safe and in my mind I was regretting to have agreed to Eric's request.

'How can we be sure that it is a Syrian mine and not one of yours? Unless we had a really close look, really up close, who can tell, right?'

I replied sardonically but the driver did not laugh. I hadn't seen a more expressionless face throughout the journey from the Fik airfield.

Little did I realise at the time that the joke was on me.

023 - Onward to A'zaz – II

Several days elapsed before I could make contact with Eric at the fenced off oil exploration compound which was guarded like a fortress by the security. One of the rooms had a satellite link that allowed video chats via Skype and the uplink was quite patchy. Telecommunications in this part of the world was quite frugal almost as if to imply that words and communication were secondary to action. None of the locals actually spoke to us or the security, even in this part of the world where time seemed to grind to a standstill, the willingness to talk and communicate seemed secondary.

'How are you finding the exploration, Len? Do you have an estimate of the oil and gas finds yet?'

I wasn't quite sure why the conversation could not begin with the usual pleasantries like 'How are you settling on around there?' or just the usual 'Good Afternoon'.
Having known Eric for several years, he was always straight to the point but despite the obvious dangers that hadn't disclosed while selling the assignment to Len, I doubt he ever considered the human costs of running the business when Innofuel's interests were hanging in the balance.

'Do you want the volume estimate or the value estimate, Eric? I believe the latter will interest you more. Fifty Billion US dollars' worth of natural petroleum reserves untapped and as yet globally unknown. This is quite a find, although I would recommend moving the natural fuel to Cyprus first then refine for shipping to base if we wish to control costs and the protection of our equipment and assets.'

'Fifty Billion?! Len, take the rest of the day off, this is tremendous! Did you see any Russian envoys in the area, any suspicious activity around the fields? It is quite key that we keep them off this find. Russia may not be able to claim the find but it will try every bit to destroy it!'

'No, Eric. This is Israeli soil and they wouldn't dare involve the communists. They need us to keep the Syrians at a distance and now they want to profit off the region too. Have you been here before, Eric?'

'No and I hope I won't have to. Keeping away from that conflict works best for us, and for you Len! You are coming back by the next available flight home, I will keep my end of the deal as promised.'

'Eric, you sent me as your foot soldier to minimise collateral in case the whole exploration went South, didn't you?'

'Len, you volunteered, remember? Besides you know the language and the people! Who else would be better suited for this?'

'I want to come back, Eric. Three miles down south, there are Syrian tanks and up on the eastern side we have Al Nusra with their ammo shelters. How come none of this gets reported on the news? This is a war zone, I can't be here, Eric!'

'Then finish the report as soon as possible, this is the job you started out to do: finish and come back, Len. What you are doing over there is historic and the US government's got your back! Am bringing up your promotion in the next board meeting. Good work, Len.'

Eric's implying we were under the 'protection' of the U.S. government did not put me at ease. We hadn't seen a single American soldier around here, maybe they were securing the region by proxy but the tentative peace was on a very delicate balance.

'Okay, I will fax in the larger details. Talk to you later, Eric.'

'Len, when you finish I will ensure you get what you asked for. Finish this and come home.'

Turning off the video link, I went back to the living quarters to find Sara trying out a heavy black burqa. It appeared to me that it would be impossible to make out if there was an armed man in there or a woman. My nerves were shot and I realised my paranoia was feeding into the discussion I just had with Eric.

'How do I look?' Sara spread out her hands and had a comic gesture: she was actually loving this.

'Like some jihadi wearing a black onesie with a bad-ass hoodie mask. Actually, not bad except am not sure what I am looking at?'

Sara paused her theatrics for once, pulled her veil aside looking intently at Len.

'You know am doing this for our safety, Len? The hijab actually makes me feel quite safe in this place. Did you have your meeting with Eric, what did he say?'

'Yes, I did. This is going to be over soon, Sara. Though Eric didn't think much to send me here he is keen to keep his end of the deal. We are going back home as soon as the travel documents arrive, fancy that!'

'We will be in London, together? Len, this is it, we will start living on our own terms. I can't believe this is happening!

Sara had tears in her eyes, she desperately wanted to get out of here and now the good news meant a turning of a new page in our lives.

'I might get promoted but I have got to finish my report and fax it out now.'

I hurried back to my desk and in almost a split moment I heard a surging shriek of a whistle through the air followed by a loud boom in front of our compound. It was a mortar shell that exploded deafening us temporarily. Concrete brick and mortar rained down on me and I blacked out for a few seconds due to the shock.

'Len, get up! Help somebody', Sara's voice sounded distant. Determined to follow the voice, I looked around to find the wall had collapsed on the desk of what my study used to be.

'My report, I need my report.' I pulled the hard bound little notepad borrowed from Innofuel stationery the other day. I carried with me and put it in my left pocket with my other arm around Sara.

We were being led outside into a smaller army truck and I saw the full scale of the damage.

Syrian tanks had entered into the lower ground partially obscured by the ridges of the Heights had fired perfect shots at the fenced off exploration area. Most of the equipment had been hit by shells, the main office was on fire. Just at the moment, we saw a smaller truck skid towards the under construction refinery from the main road.

A split second later the refinery exploded with debris thrown about a hundred feet in the air. The blast of air from the explosion landed us flat on the ground.

I looked at Sara, tears were welling up in my eyes. I brought this to her, she shouldn't have had to see this. With one mighty try I heaved up and led Sara into the truck.

'Stay here, Sara! I will be back!' I had to get back to get our passports from our now destroyed residential block.

'It is no use, Len! We save ourselves now and there might be a chance to go back home, if at all!' Sara read my thoughts, tears streaming down her face.

The Army convoy started up and we left the burning compound behind, greeted by the icy evening winds towards the Fik airstrip.

024 – Onward to A'zaz – III

The desert night was freezing cold and Sara was lucky to be
wearing the hijab which protected her not only from the cold but
from any visual observation. At this point the truck rolled to a
halt behind a dune which obstructed any view of the wasteland
for miles.

'Sir, please keep these provisions with you from now on!'
The soldier gave me a knapsack which was fairly heavy. On
opening the bag I found a pair of local Arabic garb, a hijab, some
dates and dry fruits and two bottles of water. My head was still
reeling from the explosion within the office and the soldier's
instructions made no sense to my catatonic state of mind. I had a
numbing feeling of being abandoned and left behind, part of me
didn't want me to believe what I knew was about to hear.

'What is this? Aren't you taking us to the airplane?'
A sinking feeling entered my stomach as the provisions meant at
some point we would be on our own, why else would the army
give us provisions?
'This is for you and your wife, sir. If we are ambushed and find
no way to escape, we will not surrender. However, as you are
civilians caught in the cross fire, we would attempt to provide
safe passage to you by whatever means necessary! Please change

your clothes now, Sir, just to be prepared. Do we have a heading, general?'

The group leader shook his head and pointed to the small group of Syrian foot soldiers who were torching the watch tower at the airstrip. We had lost any possibility of an aerial flight from the Wik Airstrip. The Syrian army had destroyed the ATC tower and they would almost certainly shoot down anything that flew from there.

With a solemn look on his face, the leader turned back to us addressing me in a desolate tone. We knew this was not going as planned, not even by their best laid out contingency plans.

'Sir, we will continue on the ground. Those tanks will bullet our flight from the sky! We have better chances here on the ground.'

He gave a gentle squeeze in the arm, though at the time I could barely make out the danger I had put myself and Sara into. I nodded as I changed into the clothes of a local villager. This clearly meant that we wouldn't be having a safe passage by flight definitely no fortunate escape into sovereign lands. My helpless anger at Eric increased and I made an oath in my heart to meet him once again, to show him what it really meant to be unfairly endangered in a country far from home. But inside me a truth shattered my rage: no one actually put me to it, I had volunteered. Coming here was my decision, I had no one to blame but myself.

'Please let Sara be safe, my lord. Let her not suffer as a result of my choices!'

The truck turned around away from the air strip deeper inland, the driver driving purely on instinct. The ammo on the soldiers was skeletal as this was a rescue mission and the flight from an ambush would be given priority to fight.

Sara fell asleep on my shoulder exhausted, she was shivering as I held her tight. After several hours of driving through the dark, the truck stopped. My eyes were tired of straining at the horizon looking into the desert for possible counter strike groups. Soon a herd of camel bearers met us at the road and the group leader met with the one man leading them.

The group leader came running back to me, his face streaked with sweat and worry.

'Sir, if you stay with us, you will be captured and punished by the army. We fear not our own lives but are responsible for yours. These are the Bedouin travelling over to the nearest village, Qatmah. The 'brotherhood' will rescue you from Qatmah as we will head out of here else we fear being detected by the army patrols. Word is out on the Syrian radio to capture the employees of the oil field to make an example of them: I am sorry Sir, but you are no longer safe with us!'

These men were the last clutches of straw I was holding on to as I felt the desert consume me and Sara. Realising there was no other option, I felt sinking into a depressive stupor and gently lifted my wife and myself atop a camel as were gently herded into the dusk. The Bedouin were rough in manner but they were generous at heart as they gave us some protection for the night's journey in the form of blankets. The depth of the tragic circumstances had not sunk into me completely as I just did what had to be done at the time.

'Sir, you will be fine, I have kept a telephone number in the bag. Qatmah has only one or two places from where you can buy a cell phone. Buy one and give a call as soon as you are safe. They will come to escort you out into the safe zone to the embassy. I am sorry to have to leave you and ma'am in this state but we must bid farewell for our own good!'

The truck left and soon disappeared into the dust like the last light in the blinding darkness of the night. Unfortunately for myself, everything went black too as I slumped over the camel who gently took us deeper into the barren wastelands.

As it all happened quite suddenly, I had no notion of where we were going, except that we were going to a village named Qatmah.
Soon, I dreamt of being back in London with Sara, everything was back to normal: Sara was at home, she was making my favourite mushroom soup and golden yolk poached eggs. It was all ok, she told me. We will be fine.
It was a dream, one that I didn't feel like waking from and I didn't, I was happy in that moment.

025 - Onward to A'zaz – IV

I remember Len Berkowicz as a completely different person than
Naim Nasser. Len was my past, Naim is my present.

Len was weak, ordinary and prone to being careless because he
was not cynical. There were much happier moments in his life
which made him believe in the company of men and the
optimism grew as destiny showered her luck on him. Marrying
Sara was the best thing he ever did in his life though Sara herself
should have known better than to let his will overrule her own
sometimes.
Sara loved Len totally and her submission to Len was her way of
letting Len know what he meant to her, how much she loved
him.

'Sara, did you marry an unworthy fool to have brought you into a
life changing situation such as this? Another life, another date
and another guy would have kept you safe from harm! What can
I possibly do to make this better?'
I thought as the memory of those months came back to me as we
wandered for days through the desert with the Bedouin.

Len had completely lost faith in everyone, everyone except Sara
whom he fiercely protected even from the inquisitive eyes of the
Bedouin. The wandering tribe had already realised that the petite
burqa clad woman with me was neither Arab nor of the region as
they whispered 'foreigner' in Arabic amongst themselves.

Bedouin women and men alike would come forward to help her when she could but Sara just kept crying. Her trust in me was broken: it was my decision to come here, I had never told her. Despite this she had agreed and hoped all would be ok as I had said it would be.

Sadly, the intensity of affection between one lover is never equalled by the other. Len felt Sara's love for him turn to ebb and flow as the waxing and waning of the moon. Here we were in the desert, fleeing an enemy we didn't know, not sure whether we would live the next hour. The comfortable bed in our London pad replaced by the dusty sandy bed of the desert. The dream: It had all come crashing down so quickly like sheer glass since we landed here.

'Len, water, please get some water!' Sara pleaded me through the burqa as we walked by the camels, instead of riding them. It had been weeks since we had been riding with the diminutive group of nomads. They uttered not a single complaint, happily sharing with us some water and dates when they could. It kept us going but Sara decided to walk instead for some time in the morning sun.

The events at the oilfield were still playing in my mind. I remember as I walked towards my study within the compound, the unmistakable whistle of the mortal shell. Nothing could terrorise me more than that sound. That and the blinding flash had changed me forever. Naim was already impregnated within Len from then on although at the time Len was afraid, desolate and had lost all hope of surviving through the long weeks in the sandy flat lands.

Len had grown more resolute since then, the elapsed weeks hardened him to the tough circumstances.

'Will anyone come looking for us, Len? The caliphate always look for 'tourist' trophies from the west, don't they?'

Sara had noticed Len hardening over the weeks and this bothered her. Will he remain her loved Len after this ordeal or would it change him to an un-recognisable repentant bitter and harsh person? She was worried and had always wished him to never change and be the same wonderful self whom she loved at first sight.

'No one will capture us, we would have been if the army meant to capture us. I have been thinking: did the combined intelligence of the Israeli army and the West not know of this attack? Why weren't we warned and why did the convoy leader mention the 'brotherhood' would contact us at Qatmah?'

'Len, you are trying to connect it all to a conspiracy that does not exist! None of this was meant to happen to us. None of this would have happened had I never agreed with you in the first place.'

A part of Len had died thinking about that exact last statement ever since they had fled the exploration grounds. Sara's comment came at a time when his perception was already tainted with hopelessness, rage and a thirst for revenge. He was ready for a bit of the savage treatment to be meted out to Eric had he met him now.

Naim would have never had wanted revenge like the way Len did. Still, Len was in a state of change in such bleak circumstances. Who could blame him? Their fate lay in Len's hands and he could not give himself into rage and despair.

'I hadn't thought through my decision to come here, Sara. You know my reasons to choose this last overseas assignment from Eric was driven by the thought of us being together. No more late night flights and so that I could stay in bed with you on a late Monday morning instead of hurdling over back to the airport at dawn! I will make this right, I promise. Just rest, we can't be far from the village where i will attempt contact for help.' Hopeful thoughts drifted in to shifting sands as we gently rolled into Qatmah, a land we had never heard of or known about until now.

I intently looked at the horizon as we slowly lead our way to a distant set of mud huts. This was Qatmah, our destination.

Time flies as I think of that first glance at the village five years ago, Qatmah seemed so far away yet some brief happy memories set my pace faster towards A'zaz today. All these memories tore into my soul and the pain of my physical wounds incurred in years of planned combat seemed secondary.

'Sara, I have to find you, I must see you and tell you how much I have wronged you. Long have I made you wait, please stay as you were or my heart would break.'

I said a prayer as I slowly made my way slipping through the dark and ruined western suburb of the city of Aleppo and Ahmed's eyes sneaked into my conscience. Farewell Ahmed, my friend. I hope to see you again and ask for your forgiveness. You should have met my son and Sara, someday I hope. If not, sure am I to meet a wonderful friend like you in heaven. My friend, wish me well for years have passed, millions have died, yet I make my way to meet my family and try and do the impossible.

There was but a faint hope that Sara and our son were still alive and safe in A'zaz. Plenty have died due to repeated army air strikes in these years but rumours of a remote settlement of hostages had always been making the rounds in Mahmud's camp.

'Please, God. Let them live, I love them, my life would pass to the void if I don't meet them again in A'zaz!'

026 - Onward to A'zaz – V

'My unborn son, know this that I have loved you even before you were born. I had hoped to make your landing on this life a lot smoother, surrounded by your mother's family and mine. They would have looked at your beautiful eyes and kissed your cheeks, showered you with gifts.

Yet you are to be born to loving parents in a strange land, on a dusty heathen hut with none of the luxuries you could have but with all the love of your parents who would protect you and keep you safe with the last breath of their lives.'

My thoughts kept going back to baby Omar as I made my way through the final set of blocks in the destroyed city. No one had intercepted my path, not even the Russians who probably did not consider worth the effort of sniping at a solitary rebel who seemed keener to hide than attack them.

Keeping close to Gazi Ayntap Avenue road on Route 214, the motorway which would lead through several cities, this was the shortest route of about sixty miles to A'zaz I could remember seeing on a map when planning this day for the last five years.

Having walked for days as part of my training with the rebels, I was content in keeping safe by staying away from the main motorway and keeping to the waste lands and the fields to cover my eighteen hour journey to A'zaz.

My mind wandered back to the time when Sara and Len had reached Qatmah. Len thanked the Bedouin by handing the nomadic chief his Swiss watch to 'keep the time' as he explained to the chief. Not much of a talker, the chief just smiled at Len and gave his shoulder a warm squeeze as he left without a word. In his left tunic pocket he had a cell phone with a sim that would not operate in these Syrian borders. He had hoped to be able to procure a local sim to call the embassy and the 'brotherhood' requesting a safe extraction back home.

Once in the village, Sara tried to communicate with some of the village women in the limited Arabic she had learnt since we had landed at the Golan Heights. One of them took a liking to Sara and invited her to stay in her hut. I was happy that Sara had found a place to rest and ran back to a small broken down shop for a local sim to urgently call the embassy.

'Hi, this is Len. I worked for Innofuel under Eric Leighton at the Golan Heights oil fields. We were ambushed by the Syrian Army and had to escape back into the country side to avoid getting killed, even the security left us in the protection of the wandering Bedouin. Could you please inform that Len and Sara from the UK are still alive and are now safe at Qatmah? Could you ask them of a possible extraction site for us? We have been through a lot as civilians, we are good to leave now, please help!'

'Am not sure what you are saying, Sir. Reports we have mention that Len and Sara had died in the attack at the exploration area.'

The fake news stunned me and angered me as I tried to reason who would have decided to deny that we had indeed survived? Surely one from the army protection team would have reported how we escaped with the Bedouin?

'No, there has been some confusion, we are very much alive though miles into Syrian territory. An Israeli convoy dropped us at the farthest site from the ambush.'

'Please hold, Sir.' the operator on the other end made Len wait what seemed to be forever.
'Sir, we will contact you through our local officials to verify your identity'

'Ok, when will we be able to get back home? Please, I beg you, can you ask this of the embassy?'

'Sir, you are deep into hostile territory, we cannot be certain we can extract you and your wife. Attempting to leave the village during the conflict is also not advisable, sir. I repeat, please do not attempt to leave until the local contact reaches Qatmah to provide further instructions.'

The line went dead, Len realised that this was the depth-less pit of his worst nightmares. There was no easy exit from Qatmah despite being possibly the most nondescript location on the face of the earth. Denying them their true identity, the West had sealed the fate of both Len and Sara, there was no turning back to where they had come from.

I remember how months went by, every punishingly hot day followed by the bone chilling night. The hope in Sara's eyes dimmed a little every day, the feeling of being marooned in

Qatmah changed us. Sara had found favour with the local village women who even offered her to sleep indoors in their huts. She had grown distant from Len, though in her heart she blamed Len only for his hasty decisions not for the state they were in. Neither of them could see this coming let alone take refuge in a village the world hadn't heard of. Len helped the local mosque, kept it clean and instead found refuge among the generous elders of the village.

I called the brotherhood one last time at the point of all lost hope.

'Hello, Len. Glad you could make the village and save your lives. No one could believe you could make it this far. Our sources tell us you have even blended into the village folk quite well now. Let's set aside your rescue extraction aside for a moment and talk about that.'

I was enraged by the cool voice on the other side patronising us as if our lives didn't matter. However, I didn't say a word.

The voice continued, 'I know this is the last thing you want to hear but when you volunteered for InnoFuel's project on the ground, you had been made a part of the western alliance's mission to have 'eyes on the ground' What about human rights, you would say? Dead people have no rights, Len. To get you out of there, we need your help. Give us a call every Saturday after the evening prayer is over.'

The condescension is his tone enraged me but I had to listen. This was a number provided by the Israeli commander before they abandoned us, there was no telling who was on the other side of the phone? Were they slave traders, were they CIA? I had no idea and I dared not antagonise the voice at the other end.

'Remember Len, Qatmah has no television, radio, telephones or the internet and people do drop like flies as they would in the desert. If you co-operate, we might be able to help you but until then you and Sara need to keep from being dead.'

I had no pride left to protest, instead the prospect of giving hope to Sara brought back some life within myself and I found myself with moist eyes.

'What do you want me to do?'

'Len, you will report to me. You won't know my name because we will never meet personally but do not give this number to anyone in the desert. Be assured I will find you and behead you and your wife at the market square if you do! IF I were you, I would change that name and convert to Islam to survive there.'

I was a proud Jew and the suggestion enraged me but I had little choice but to listen and ask

'How long will we be here?'

'Possibly months, though you could escape earlier if you do exactly as I say! The Syrian army frequently form local alliances with groups to protect their borders. Unfortunately, some of them are our own brother rebels! Curse those infidels! They will visit your village every now and then. Observe, try and get names and report to me every week even if they don't through!'

'I need money.' My pride had died the day since I couldn't provide for Sara living at the generosity of the local womenfolk, I begged without resent. I really needed to be able to provide for the both of us.

'Len, there is a sum of money arranged with the local elder, Mahmud. Go take it from him today after the evening prayer. Mahmud will make you an offer that you would be foolish to refuse. Humor him as much as you can, help is coming.'

The line went dead. Never had I felt more hopeless and in utter lack of control over my destiny. I sat down outside the telephone shop contemplating the hope that Sara had for so long let go. What would I not do to make her smile , have some hope in her eyes, just to see the Sara I knew if only for a moment?

027 - Onward to A'zaz – VI

Mahmud Nasser was a kind quiet spoken elder of the village who was respected for being fair and generous to the villagers of Qatmah. But one only needed to bring a 'traitor' to his presence that could transform Nasser from the amiable elder to the fearsome vanguard, judge, jury and executioner of harsh justice.

I was the invisible hand, the informer of such traitors to Mahmud. These were mostly uncouth rough and Godless men who had no intention but to profit off the spoils of war and had defected to the Syrian army when they found out the rebels had little means to get by in their daily lives. The American army hadn't joined the fray then, hadn't become brothers with the locals then to fight this war. They were still deciding the cost and the profit of 'their' war in the pentagon board rooms with oil and gas powerhouses lobbying for their involvement.

Often the execution of these loathsome men was at the village market center. Kids as young as five years old would come over to view the beheadings up close. At a time there would be up to three executions bleeding up the market sands, these cursed men awaiting their fate would look upon the pile of wood on which their comrades would be roughly piled. They knew they were next and in a moment they would pass into the unknown with their severed heads placed unsympathetically on their chest. No Islamic burial for these traitors, just the fire on the pier the smoke of which would signal far and wide to friends and foes alike just what Mahmud Nasser would do to those who were 'traitors' to the free people.

'Do you think of me as an evil man, Len?'
Mahmud asked me one afternoon after the executions with an honesty and earnestness I had never heard before.

'No, sire. You do what you believe in, your principles and your convictions are for the freedom of the people here and your actions an example for your enemies. Let them quake in fear, sir, God knows they deserve it!'

'Sit down Len, have some tea with me, come.'

As I sat down with the towering Arab elder, I noticed Mahmud had plenty of heavy guns in his tent and his men guarded them at all times.

'Len, I would only wish their respect and not their lives to me, to the people of this village. There is no single just side in our conflict, we have let our emotions loose like a pack of rabid dogs, my friend! We have fought before, us, the Kurds, your people the Iranians, the Iraqis. We have been fighting since the demise of Babylonia and the fall of the great Arab kingdoms but we have lost our honour in the way we fight today. But there is no side to this fight who is good or bad, no single winner or loser. We are all losers, those who destroy the spirit of our people and we who destroy symbols of what they believe in such as sacred grounds, Len. This used to be an engagement of rules that defined the wars on principles. We used to have respect for our enemies but with that missing from our conflict both sides know this will end in a stalemate with very little left to live, die or fight for.'

Mahmud had tears in his eyes, for the first time I felt he had a trace of guilt behind his righteousness and ruthless nature. He looked at me briefly then up at his decorative carpets sprawling in his spacious room and continued in the same sombre note.

'The west whom all Arabs have thought our allies and I do not just refer to Qatmah, the rebels or even our enemy, the dictator dynasty sitting at the heart of this country. That is our enemy, Len, the governments where you come from! Had the west treated us as their equals, not manipulated us for pure greed of our resources. They have set the fire and who amongst the corrupted lot amongst us can put it out?'

There was a fair point to Mahmud's point of view. I was brought as part of that plan to exploit the beautiful land of Golan Heights to dig up the land for oil and gas. It was irrelevant to such powerful western entities whom the wealth belonged to. These entities belonged to a powerful syndicate, an association more powerful than governments. As I realised later: Never seen, never heard and never talked about, they never respected the countries they did business with, in fact the commerce was not their business. The syndicate made the stately affairs of these countries their business. A game played at a level unimaginable by ordinary citizens and I was now a part of them.

To discover this syndicate you would need to be staring into the murkiest portals of human history. But the knowledge of the syndicate changed me completely, left me in a dark place full of helpless rage and anger. I didn't feel in control of my destiny, worse, it was not in the hands of my God but in the crafty hands of the syndicate. But I was quite naive then and oblivious of this all powerful mortal entity.

'Sire, I only pray for this conflict to end. It has been ten months since I have been your humble and hardworking guest. My wife and I now live by your grace under one roof and we have our baby, Omar who has already taken after his mother and father's sense of the correct way of life. All this by your grace, sire.'

I kissed Mahmud's hand in genuine reverence.

'Len, my son, for your own safety maybe it's time for a change in your name. Shall we call you Naim of Qatmah? Oh, it could not be better! Naim! After my own reverential teacher and knowledge seeker! You are no more Len, but Naim Nasser!'

I was initially bewildered by his impromptu christening but I actually felt much relaxed with this new identity. My baptism at the hands of a man whom I respected for his generosity, a relief that Len can finally die after all the pain and trauma he had gone through.

Strangely enough, like a shadow that followed me until now graciously retreated in a corner of my eye, smiling. He was tired, tired was Len and happy that I was finally letting him go in peace. I was exhilarated and left for home after thanking Mahmud for this afternoon that would change my life forever.

'Len, I haven't seen you so peaceful in years, what is the matter?' Sara asked me as she nursed baby Omar in her arms.

'I am Naim Nasser, Sara. Len had to leave.'

Sara looked at me incredulously, I kissed her, hugged our future, Omar. I felt accepted, felt like I finally belonged to this harsh unyielding land. It had been a year and while this was no modern western city, we were transformed by the peace-loving pure people of the village. No psychiatrist, no medication or western medicine could heal us in the same manner as our stay at Qatmah had done in the last twelve months. I was born, again.

028 - Onward to A'zaz – VII

'Happiness, what are you but a fickle friend of mine, observing
me from the dunes, smiling?
Come, would you not stay for a while with me and my family?
Where forth do you go, why do you leave?'

The song of the travelling Bedouin would stay in our minds and
hearts long after they graciously rescued us from certain death.
More than a year had passed peacefully since I had reached
Qatmah with little hope of surviving more than a few days. Fate,
it seemed had planned a better future for us though not without
a sense of irony.

Bidding a fond farewell to Len, I was happy with my family
finding new meaning in life being a father to baby Omar. Omar,
you little brat.
'How many times do you make your father change your
underclothes, kid?'
I would mentally ask Omar often wondering how lucky I was to
be able to do this and still continue providing my humble
services to Mahmud.

'Naim, it is time for Omar's milk, bring him over...Omar, you
will take a bath after your feed, boy! You need a proper cleaning.'

Sara breastfed the already ravenous Omar and looked at me with contentment. Never had I felt at peace as of this moment, my mind created a special place of this moment in my mind, in my heart. The three of us, happy, content and peaceful.

Outside not far away arose a slight row among a crowd, followed by rapid fire assault gunfire piercing the peaceful air of Qatmah. Many village men including myself came outside to see what or who caused the uproar.

To my horror I realised the inevitable had happened: Qatmah was overrun by Syrian army soldiers led by a much feared general who went by the name of Salem. There were about a few hundred in bright army green holding the heads of a few of the rebel guards protecting the village. Heads of men I knew and shared my evening tea with. I was enraged yet the sight of the odd hundred struck fear in my heart. I observed quietly as the men swung the dismembered heads towards frightened children and their mothers who retreated to the comfort of their homes.

The Army General came to the front with a fistful of my friend's heads and addressed the villagers with the nonchalance that unnerved me to the core. Cold and personal revenge was to be served today as he spoke with a measured calm.

'Villagers of Qatmah, many a times you have burnt my men on this market pyre. They were ruthless to your folk and so you killed them, I can understand. For the sake of justice your men will burn here this time so this 'holy' pyre is really a sacrificial altar. Now soldiers, enemy or friend, must burn here!'

Salem patted the pyre as if it were the back of a healthy farm horse, smiling all the while as his menacing eyes searched the crowd. He was looking for someone.

'Now where is that coward, Mahmud Nasser? Where are you hiding him? Hand him over to me and we will leave at once, I give me word.'

Mahmud was hiding in plain sight, standing among the villagers looking at the army numbers. Knowing him I knew he was trying to figure out a way to summon an evasive action and get the hidden ammunition from inside his tent.

All of Qatmah lay silent, refusing to let their leader be taken by the hands of the enemy. Every one of us loved Mahmud much more than ourselves to hand him over. It was quite evident to me over time that Mahmud had won over the village with love and respect not fear.

'Mahmud is all of us, not one, Sire. Please, we offer you our hospitality and an opportunity to sit down and discuss as equals. Your men with our men. Please, sire.'

To our astonishment we realised it was the voice of Mahmud's youngest daughter. My heart went cold with dread but melted at the warmth of this beautiful warm innocent child who wanted nothing but the peace between the elders. Pure heart, bless her soul, she stepped to the army general with a desert rose in her hand.

Quite shocked and not quite expecting the honesty of the child, Salem awkwardly looked at the kid, slowly bent down on his knees to have a good look at her through her veil. For a moment,

Mahmud's youngest peered at the general's eyes as her arm outstretched a rose to his face.

Then the unthinkable happened and I wish I had died rather than see it happen. The army general flipped his service revolver from his hip holster and shot the angel right through her face. Was this a nightmare I keep questioning myself to this day. Could I ever change this dreadful moment, I wonder? Could I ever do anything at all to turn this moment and save her? The world crashed around us, our body and soul unsure how to react to this sudden shocking instant.

Shrieks and wails rose from the villagers as I looked at Mahmud whose mouth was open, the sudden tragedy gave him no moment to shed a tear. The suddenness of the brutal murder hadn't sunk into all of us as our consciousness grappled with the abrupt nature of the execution of Mahmud's youngest.

'Take all the women out!! You infidels will pay for your insolence and be shamed as we take your women with us! Your women will leave with us! Take them out! And take these bodies including this stupid girl here and toss them onto the pyre! Get the fire ready!'

With horror I looked at Sara, who looked at me with those same terror filled eyes, speaking in unspoken words.

'Len, do something, please! Don't let them take us. What about Omar, will we survive? Please don't let them take me! I can't do this without you, save our Omar, please. Take him with you even if I have to leave, Naim, he is too young to survive this!'

135

All those pleas not uttered by Sara, only communicated by her eyes pierced me like a thousand knives. With teary eyes, I looked at Mahmud begging for action. Mahmud already shaken as his tragedy sunk upon him like a lead weight motioned me to stay where I was.

'Naim! Naim! ' , Sara could only manage to call out my name, she was crying uncontrollably, baby Omar in hand who started crying as the soldier pulling at her roughly. Within a few minutes all the women in their hijab had been rounded up.

'Why wouldn't Mahmud do nothing?!'
I wondered, my eyes shifting wildly from Mahmud to the retreating hostages.

'We keep your treasures with us, you kaffirs! Unless you surrender your boys and men to us, you may never see your women and children again! Come on men, onward to A'zaz! And someone light that pyre!!'

Time lapsed as I froze on the ground I stood all this while, unable to comprehend what had we possibly done to deserve such a fate? Mahmud looked at the pyre, rooted in the ground in the exact same manner as I was. His baby girl was burning on the pyre, her beautiful white feet stuck out of the flames, as if in defiance for her righteousness and her wish to make peace even in the face of violence.

'Mahmud, why did you stop me from picking weapons?! Why did you not do anything, sire?! Why?'

Mahmud transformed from his frozen form into the emotional mentor I had seen when he christened me. Holding me by my arms, he said words I would never forget.

'Naim! Look over there on the pyre! That's my Noor on the pyre as the flames consume her! See how her unburnt feet points in defiance towards us! What does this mean, Naim? Violence is a recourse taken only to ensure peace, not more violence!! Look around you, if we took those guns out and retaliated all of us would be dead when the army returned fire. It would be all over. We will live to fight another day to claim back whom we love and have lost! Our sons are here, their fathers too! We will free them, Naim. Inshallah!'

At the last sentence, Mahmud could no longer continue but fell on my shoulder crying. I couldn't quite put in words how I felt or what I was going through at the time except for an acute sense of loss and despair.

Both of us fell on the market floor, our eyes to the sky darkening to a chilly night as the gentle weeping of the women faded away from the streets of Qatmah.

029 – Onward to A'zaz VIII

The sun had started to rise as I made the final leg of the journey towards A'zaz. The crack of dawn helped me clear up my thoughts after my herculean effort to try and remember every moment of my life since I made the fatal decision to accept Eric's proposition to work at the Golan Heights exploration project.

I decided to stay well clear off Route 214 which would be a more direct route to A'zaz but would be more guarded by the Al-Nusra who commanded control of the town, the other remaining half commanded by my 'comrades', the FSA.

My thoughts drifted to Eric. The man with a plan who had the distinguished demeanour of a gentleman but by his actions, a ruthless savage. Len would have been apprehensive of approaching Eric, would have avoided confronting the men responsible for changing his and Sara's lives forever.

However, as Naim I had little left to fear having lost so much. Forged from the harsh desert sands, having survived miraculously at a distant Arabic village which the world had never heard of, I was as patient as a tracking tiger out for its prey.

The one memory of a singular event, that of losing my wife and son could make my hands tremble but I would steady them with the hope that I would rescue them when they were taken away on that fateful day.

Mahmud, our elder and our leader whom we report to after every mission keeps reminding me with moist eyes that they are still alive, and for them it is why I fight with my brothers.

What I distinctly remember was a part of the army had come back that day when our wives and daughters were taken hostage. They wanted more as a strange rage I noticed in those army men who kicked and abused their victims even after they were long dead.

We hid inside our houses until we were sure that they had left and it is at this point the army returned and started to set the roofs of the village huts on fire.

Soon, screams of pain emerged from the burning houses as I hid in a toilet hole at the extreme end of our house. I could only see the bright orange light emitted by the hot flames as it fed on the dry straws on the roof of the neighbouring house.

'This one! Who has left this one? Burn it down!'

I had a sinking feeling in my stomach, this was someone asking my house to be torched.

'There is someone in there, I can hear it! Get out, you infidel! Show whom you shelter!'

Worried as I was, I was hoping that the 'brotherhood' would come around to help us. For better or for worse I was still carrying out orders that served me as it served them. Surely, they would evacuate or rescue us this time?

'All right, burn it down! Start with the roof up front!'

At this I covered the pit with the slab as the heat started to permeate through the slab and it started getting hot.

'It's too late!' I touched the slab to move it. I had to get out of here or risk being baked alive.
The slab was already too hot and my fingertips burned. Wincing from the pain, I have a push with my knuckles and shoved it aside enough to be able to come out of the dirty pit. It was getting hotter as the burning roof started to rain down fire.
By now the pit had become a cauldron of fire and I came out to realise my shoulders were burnt to the skin, my feet were completely black, sore and bleeding: escape was impossible with me injured this badly.

The 'brotherhood' still had not arrived by then, I was desperate to find any hole deep enough for me to hide until the army left. There was nowhere else to go, the whole village had been torched, some still with children trapped inside. Some of the army men tried to take out the children but the little ones were too afraid and refused to come out: they had seen the brutality of the army and dreaded their treatment if they did come out.

Covering myself with a thick blanket, I had to crawl down back into the smouldering hot pit. The blanket prevented my skin from burning instantly but the heat melted the blanket to my back. After some time the military left, I came out with the blanket still stuck to my burnt back and passed out on the ground behind my house.

Sweet dreams of meeting my wife and son at A'zaz filled my senses, I could feel the warmth of their cheeks on mine. The last I heard the group of Qatmah's women and their babies were abandoned in A'zaz under a regime of mercenaries.

'When are you coming for us, Naim? Omar is frail, I need you.'

At some point after escaping the red hot toilet pit at the back of my torched hut, Mahmud Nasser had come across with a few men. He looked at me and broke into tears but quickly dried his eyes and ordered his men to pick me up for treatment.

'What is happening to me, Mahmud? Am I going to die?'

Mahmud looked at me and touched my forehead, his eyes starting to well up again.

'Inshallah, Naim. You will live to avenge this day! Now rest my son, it is a long journey. We will talk when you are treated from this ghastly burns.'

I felt I was in a vehicle, gently rolling away from the torched village, the sound of crackling fire consuming the huts slowly left me.

For days I found it hard to breathe as I felt bandaged from head to toe, reeking of antiseptic and medicine. Alas, no morphine for the pain as it felt like a thousand spikes tearing at my rotting flesh.
'Adonai..', I cried out when they changed my bandages. The words stopped the men but Mahmud would urge them to finish their task.

Six Months later, my bandages came off. Mahmud looked at me and smiled, I hadn't seen him for most of these months as I recovered. His persona had changed: though he was still very much the elder among the rebel group he was now also their field leader on ground operations. In better times, Mahmud would run his plans from his home in Qatmah, now he went into the fields himself with his men.

'Naim, you are healed my son! Physically at least, like the rest of us.'

He held a mirror to my face and body showing me my scars from the fire which had nearly consumed me. My skin around my back, arms and tip of my ears had burnt and now healed, they appeared pink white, patch like and very soft as new skin.

'Now, Naim in your pain and suffering you called out to your lord. The boys here are aware that you are no Arab though I christened you. Some were willing to kill you but I stopped them. Your blood may be perceived as that of an enemy but I have felt your sincerity in our cause.
We spoke, debated and finally here you are treated and safe though some of my men, I admit, do despise you.
For you and for my sake, for what we have been through together at Qatmah I humbly request you, like father to son, to join our cause as an active soldier on this holy jihad. This may also be the only way you can find out and possibly rescue your one remaining link to your true self: your wife, Sara and your son, Omar!'

Their names brought a violent jolt to my eyes, filling them with hot tears. Mahmud held on to me and continued.

'Fight with me, son. You will survive and get stronger. Inshallah, you will one day rescue them too!'

My decision to join Mahmud's cause couldn't have felt more right, more appropriate. It felt and still feels as the best decision I had ever taken in my life. I hugged him in acceptance.

As we parted, Mahmud turned around and paused, weighing whether to disclose something that had been bothering him since I was conscious.

'Naim, the American government helps us several times to fight our enemy, though many times our missions aren't exactly aligned and we have to help each other at times in terms of field intelligence and fire cover. They mentioned about a man, a very powerful man in Washington asking for Len, their main man in the Golan Heights. Someone very powerful up there wants you dead!'

My tears dried up and a seething thirst for revenge filled my heart at the mention of Eric. I will take my time with him and it will be a cold plate of vengeance that I vow to carve him on when the right time came.

'Len is dead, Sire. Long ago. Make no mention of our christening, father, I beg you.'

Mahmud gave me a hug, as a father to son. He then stepped away, his demeanour changing to the sterner field officer that he presented to his group.

'You are Allah's soldier now, Naim. Keep your head high as you now fight for his cause! Be ready at the crack of dawn tomorrow

143

for we will make our mission to re-take Aleppo a success. Rest now, at ease until tomorrow!'

That was it. Mahmud had saved my life twice and I was forever indebted to him. Now five years later, as I made my detour through Minaq and Ayn Daqnah to A'zaz I walked directly towards to FSA camps that were not too far away from their fearsome foes, the Al Nusra.

Explaining to Mahmud about the unfortunate turn of events and the betrayal of Akachi would be difficult. But it would be the truth and the only protection I had against Mahmud's punishment for deserters. And that just might save my life to rescue my family from the Al-Nusra held province around the mosque of Kilis.

A lurking thought went towards Eric.
'Hold on to that thought, life is more important than death or vengeance at this time.'
I slowly made my way to the FSA camp, arms raised, standing behind a shelled hut just in case they decided to fire anyway. Urgent Arabic words were spoken and they beckoned me to come out of my hiding very slowly.

'Please, general, please allow me to speak with my master, my commander, Mahmud Nasser who at this very moment controls larger parts of eastern Aleppo!'

030 - A Maternal Transaction

'Naim Nasser! Where is Mahmud's guest? Mahmud wishes to speak to this man!'

A hush of silence fell through the ranks of the rebels as they heard my name called by their field leader. Most of them sized me up wondering how I had made the long journey to A'zaz without getting shot. Some whispered 'the stealthy snake' in Arabic as they stared in awe wondering what training I had to have survived the gruelling trek to the camp. Their leader, Mohammed led me on to where a phone was kept.

'Naim, Mahmud is on a phone call on speaker, he has been most anxious of the outcome of the mission that he sent three of his most able soldiers on. Mahmud, are you there? Naim is the one reporting from the mission, sir. He wished to speak with you privately, but my men need to know of the mission as well!'

A familiar kind voice spoke, I recognised Mahmud from the slightly distorted phone connection. Hearing of Mahmud's voice I made a silent prayer to Allah to clear my path by way of truth. I could not speak anything but the truth to Mahmud, who was more than a leader, a father to me.

145

'No, Mohammed. It is ok, you may keep the line in speaker as Naim speaks. We have nothing to hide from our brothers. Naim! You have a thousand lives, son! Tell us what came off the mission, I have two men missing and one man, like my own son, you in so far away a place as A'zaz?'

'Sire, our mission was ambushed by a team of Russian snipers, RPG attack and a subsequent betrayal doomed any chances of success. Our last point of contact was at the abandoned hotel at the market center before all hell broke loose.'

"Betrayal'?! Did you say betrayal, Naim? We will come to that after. Please continue.'

'Sire, we were an hour into our journey towards the main supply link on the eastern side of the city. Our mission to disrupt the main supply link for the army failed as we were attacked by Russian snipers before we could get to the rendezvous point.'

A murmur went through the gathered rebels, some of them stared at me with distrust. All of them had but one question in their faces: how was I the only one to survive?

'What happened to the rest of the men, Naim? I have had no contact with them nor any sign of them being alive!'

A vision of Ahmed's desolate face flashed across my eyes and my voice faltered and went low. I had to gather myself to avoid showing my personal grief to an audience who would not tolerate any sign of weakness.

'No one survived, Sire. While the Russians dropped an RPG on our truck, our driver had no time to escape. The three of us went atop a vantage point in the abandoned hotel with the Kurds. We were weakened further Akachi turned on us, Sire! He betrayed us!'

The murmur grew louder among the assembled rebels who appeared to have grown restless at the mention of 'betrayal'.

'Wait, Naim! Speak no more! Mohammed, the line is quite poor, take the call off the speaker and let Naim speak? He will report the details to you!'

Mohammed handed me the phone with reluctance and suspicion. Mahmud's voice crackled on to the phone,

'Naim! What is this? Are you saying Akachi was a traitor? You said no one had survived. Are you sure?'

'Sire, Akachi was a traitor in Timbuktu, traitor to the very principles you and I hold dear! He had murdered Ahmed's uncle in Kabara right before he was promoted by the Ansar Dine to come over here to 'help' our cause! Ahmed neutralised him before he took aim at us while we were defending ourselves against the Russians. I hadn't expected Ahmed to live, Sire. He had refused to come away with me, choosing instead to finish Akachi while taking his time with that infidel. Do you have any news of his escape or whether he lives, Sire? He was much distraught to have learnt of his Uncle Haider's fate!'

Mahmud sighed then answered in the tone Naim recognised back from the old days in Qatmah.

'Ahmed never reported back, Naim. Now I know why. He feels

betrayed by his own brothers who pledged to fight and die for the cause together. I should have known, Naim. But I assure you I did not know of Akachi's involvement with Ahmed's uncle Haider. I have lost a son in Ahmed but I will keep searching for him and bring him home.

Naim, you are so close to A'zaz? Have you given your family a thought?'

I had to be careful in my answer , I had no wish to let Mahmud know I wished to stop fighting as I had told him I would stop after I rescued my family. He wouldn't understand especially after his youngest and his favourite daughter was slaughtered by the army. War gave this once great and benevolent man some peace as it gave him a purpose to live and avenge the execution of little Noor.

'Sire, your elder daughters, possibly my wife and Omar, may still be alive within the Al - Nusra held Kilis mosque. This is recent intelligence from your own commander Mohammed. Let me lead this mission to rescue them and bring them back home. The Syrian army would be given an insult and we might see our family again giving us and our rebels at Qatmah something to rejoice over! Please, Sire. Father, please give me this one opportunity that you said you would give me when we broke down at the market sands at Qatmah!'

'Naim, we are chasing shadows trying to rescue them but I cannot go back on my word I gave you, son. But if you go there and succeed, your mission is over. You will never come back to me in order to live with your wife and son. How can I possibly survive that loss without becoming a broken man? My daughters! I would be happy to see them but you, my son, I would lose you forever!'

'Sire, no father could do what you did for me! I have been and will always be your son but for your son's wish, could you not grant me hope and closure? We will never forgive ourselves of the guilt of not having tried, father! You have yourself said I have survived many times to have a thousand lives. Was I alive so far not because I was to rescue them someday? It is Allah's will, Sire. Please give me the order.'

Mahmud's voice broke softer as he acceded to my wishes,

'Naim, our western partners are now aware of who you are, they have got their intelligence much against my wishes from lower subordinate officers within my group. You have my approval to lead a mission with Mohammed's men. But be careful of hostiles within the team as they do consist of western mercenaries who might have been given a contract on your head. You are precious, my son, and these western powers perceive you as their biggest embarrassment!
I have further bad news for you: the captured villagers have been taken further into an abandoned castle much deeper into Kilis. This mission will take you deeper into Turkish territory from which there is little hope of returning alive. They are on the Rawanda Kalesi, the winter fort deep in Kilis.
Inshallah, Naim come back with your family and with my dear daughters Soham and Fatimah!'

The line went dead. I looked at Mohammed who appeared uncomfortable but could already surmise what was the final decision on the mission.

I told him as I addressed the assembled rebels who had stood up having heard of their brother Ahmed lost in grief and revenge.

149

The looks of suspicion were gone from their faces, they were waiting to listen to me, to talk to me.

'We break at dawn in separate convoys to Kilis. For dignity of the stoic villagers of Qatmah, for the ideals of the freedom of oppression, Syed Mohammed, lead me to your team. We are going to Kilis to rescue our own people from the Syrian infidels. May Allah protect us from bullets that do not bear our name, may he give us hope when it seems to have left us. May he greet us with love when the right time comes! Allah of Akbar!'

The gathered men responded to my call, raising their rifles clamouring for strength to fight the evil in men.

031 - Smoking Tarmac to Kilis

'Kilis is not Syrian territory, Naim. Most of A'zaz's side roads and main roads have a divided control between us and the al-Nusra Front. No easy entry, yet no easy escape from here, comrade.'

My quizzical look at Mohammed made me realise that I had lost track of the rest of the world for a while. All this time an international situation had quickly developed in A'zaz. Turkey had introduced a further group of mercenaries into this once peaceful region that sheltered the refugees of other nations. A group that would fight as one of our dominant groups, the ISIS.

'They are vermins to put out fire with fire, American mercs in the mix. We know little of them and people only whisper 'Turkmen' when asked about their identities. Our best hope is we don't encounter them as their assault ammunition is recent and American, far more superior than ours.'

For what seemed an interminable amount of time as we made our way around the roundabout through the city, we kept our movements in the truck to a bare minimum, looking out for snipers. Most of A'zaz's residents stayed indoors during the day for fear of the Syrian rockets hitting stray targets. The rockets were tiny but did significant damage wherever they hit, claiming the lives of children out in the streets scrounging for supplies. A'zaz was a ghost town during the day, the streets echoed only of Al-Nusra or FSA trucks patrolling the desolate roads. By dusk, the children would cautiously patter into the streets, resuming their mission to scrounge and provide for their family, trying against all odds to make their parents proud.

Mohammed's instructions played over and over again as we went through the narrow by-lanes of A'zaz. We kept a sharp eye on open windows for possible snipers but after a while it seemed impossible to tell if those dark gutted windows were manned or unguarded.

The steady drone of the truck's engine as we made our way towards Alhdeden market, once a great market now turned to rubble. Al Nusra loyalists would be watching our every move as we moved out of the city. The uneasy truce was a delicate balance of ceasefire resting on a knife's edge in this part of the town. We just kept our eyes on the road ahead, it would take a while to cover the 47 km journey to where the hostages were imprisoned.

'Rawanda Kalesi is where all of Qatmah's many women and children are being held by a faction loyal to the Syrian Army.'

'Unbelievable! Kilis is not even Syrian territory yet they are being held by a loyal faction.'

'Plenty happens here which you are not aware of and would be shocked to hear my friend.'

Mohammed looked at me with those piercing eyes, probing, checking if my resolve to undertake this risky venture had withered. He looked away, took a swig of black coffee off his canteen staring intently at the approaching roundabout which would take us out of Kilis into route D410 leading to Musabeyli Yolu.

'Rawanda Kalesi is the northwest extreme of Kilis, Naim. No one particular force claims of any control, the Syrians have been secretly piling on their weapons while everyone focused on the civil war in nearby Aleppo. At the Turkish border of Kilis, we will have no choice but to crush border patrol completely.'

'While the border forces recover, we will head straight for our final 25 mile journey onto the foot hills of Rawanda Kalesi. Our main challenge is to radially access the fort by taking vantage points from different directions on the sides of the Afrin valley.'

'Correct, most of the refugees will be in the castle ruins. Thanks to Allah this isn't the winter time as it would get quite cold on our ascent to the castle. Naim, are you sure any of the hostages are actually alive?'

The question shook me from inside: I had no idea. I had brought these men on hope that they would rescue those hostages but we weren't sure if any had survived five bone chilling winters on top of that hill. Last night many of Mohammed's men mostly men who were fathers to their dead children volunteered to assist in this rescue mission. Fifteen fathers on a mission branded a 'lost cause' by those who chose not to join us. Some of us had family, some had lost entire families but the one thread tying us together was exactly that one single idea that we would risk it all for: family. Nasser's daughters, Sara and Omar, for the love of Ahmed's lost nephews, for Salman's revenge on the execution of his entire family of his children and their mothers. It did not matter if the mission did not involve rescuing their own, this was a rescue of their own souls, of my soul, lost in this swell of tyranny.

'Make way through Alhdeden market, cross into the city center of A'zaz: the al-Nusra wouldn't dare attack you there, it is too public and out in the open. Keep moving on to 'Ömer bİn AbdÜlAzİz Camİİ', from where the road will be deserted for a larger part of the 25 miles to Kilis. Should most of you survive up to this point, it is at Kilis you will question whether it was worth coming this far, fight the Turkish rebels to proceed deeper into the Turkish territory of Rawanda Kalesi in Kilis. Remember, Naim, do not let your ego swallow your common sense. If injuries are sustained, no doubt there will be; do not be foolish to persist unless all men could make it through to Kilis!'

Reminded of Mahmud's warning as we passed the big mound by the side of the Alhdeden market, we made our way into Kilis-Öncüpınar-Suriye Yolu under the watchful eyes of the Al-Nusra.

'Mohammed, we will need to branch out into two groups when we enter Turkey. Too much would be at stake to have casualties at the Öncüpinar border gates. We won't sustain our journey further into Kilis if we lose even one of us.'

'Naim, they would still attack us on our way back, God knows they will be prepared knowing well we have entered with no intention of staying in their wretched land! Some of us will die, a sacrifice these men are willing to make. Branching out will halve our strength in numbers: no, I cannot think any good would come off that.'

'We are not coming back, Mohammed.'

My statement took time to sink into the hardened general until he laid his piercing eyes on me.

'Naim, what words did you have with Mahmud after I spoke with him? Did I just bid my final farewell to my wife and daughter?'

Returning his gaze unflinchingly, I realised that this was a man who did not have any patience for flaky plans. Mohammed wanted to hear of my plan and he demanded my explanation without uttering as much as a sentence, not for his safety, but for the safety of the group of men under his command.

'We are not going back to A'zaz at all, if you had time to meet your family back before you left you probably met them before a longer journey back home. Mahmud did not send us on a suicide mission but a difficult, near impossible one. One that you would not deny had you felt the pain of those mothers displaced from their homes, babies at hand.'

'Naim, do not test my patience: my concern is for our men who have chosen, myself included, to assist you in your heroic but ultimately vain rescue attempt! What has Mahmud, that scheming old wolf, told you that he hasn't told me?'

'We need to go deeper into Turkey to exit back into Syria through borders less guarded. Turkish militia would expect us to be back on the same route as it is the shortest exit back to A'zaz. We will take the shortest route to safety in Sahra where Mahmud would be waiting to welcome us. From there on, a slightly longer trip for every one of us eventually back to A'zaz.'

Mohammed was impressed by the plan and the dark stare he directed at me turned earnest as stared at the road ahead. Both of us stared at the road ahead and we were looking into the future, our individual destinies would yet be so distinct but yet quite intertwined.

032 - A treacherous draw, a fateful hand

My heart was beating a lot heavier, a lot stronger as our trucks
lumbered through the sandy roads on the flats towards the
Turkish check point at Kilis. Five years I had been dreaming of
this day when the hope to meet Sara and Omar would warm my
heart which had grown cold like the winter morning hearth.
Trying to imagine the reunion was too overwhelming a thought,
one that I pushed to the back of my mind knowing well how a
dream could end up being a nightmare, one that would be
impossible to wake from if our plan failed.

'How long have you known Mahmud?'
Mohammed asked me as he found me pensively looking into the
horizon.

'Mahmud was my first step toward hoping for a new life,
Mohammed. If it weren't for him I would have been dead
already. If not for him, I would have never had a son, my wife
would never have been a mother. I owe a lot to him, more than
my allegiance, faith and gratitude.'

'There are plenty who would say that about him but know this:
Mahmud is a human being not a God, Naim. Plenty of us
worship men like him but I would say respect and gratitude is as
far as you should go. Not that I am envious of his legend but

more cautious of what worship without reason can do as it has done in our country! Ah, look we are nearly at the border!'

Mohammed looked into endless sands that met the blue sky on a barren flat land. Pointing out to a cross road about five miles away, one end of which appeared to be just a path, the other stretching further into the desert, he uttered the one word which meant preparation, 'Öncüpinar!'

Looking through my binoculars I saw about six men in Turkish fatigues, two on each side of what appeared to be a wooden check-post on the road and two more guarding the road, ready to attack or sacrifice themselves on duty.

'Kill with honour if you have to, we are going through that road, all of us: alive! Salman and Ahmed, our rifles get hot too fast so fire only if you have too. Collect their ammunition too, we will need it!'

I motioned at Salman and four others to file off the moving truck. They would flank the group off the left as would Ahmed and his four men from the right. Having fought and survived the conflict all these years one tends to realise that ammunition and guns are only a means to succeed. Instead our guns and ammunitions could fail us if our minds weren't strong enough. The mind finds strength in numbers, in the numbers of your brothers with you. A fleeting image of Ahmed passed before my eyes. He was still in my heart in every conflict as my comrade, my brother. The image shook me from within. Only two men including Mohammed and myself remained on the truck.

'Mohammed, wear these Turkish border fatigues from the ones

we captured earlier this month. Hurry before they can view our approach on their binoculars.'

Our driver had already changed into one of the battered uniforms before we left A'zaz. The worn fatigues were from the dead Turkish soldiers who were tied to rebel trucks dragging them across the desert. By all appearances we must look victorious coming back from an ambush on the rebels.

Mohammed was inflamed by the idea, but realising there was no time as the border check post would catch up on our activity from within a mile, he made haste despite loathing the very smell emanating off the uniform.

While he wore the uniform, I noticed that the Turkish border force emblem had been badly mutilated: the rebels must have stabbed the victim several times through before dragging him.

'Bloody Idiots to have put on a show like that!'
I thought as we slowed down even more on our approach to the check-post. I myself changed into Syrian fatigues as per the plan.

The breakout group of Salman and Ahmed made hefty progress like jackals surrounding a prey at the kill zone, positioning themselves just perpendicular to our approach on the eight lane border check-post. We chose Oncupinar Gumruk Kapisi primarily because this was a civilian check-post. Although thoroughly modernised with telephones and strong iron gates, Turkish forces would not expect an ambush here least of all from the rebels wearing Turkish and Syrian rags.

'Tie this rope around my left ankle, quickly!'

I tied the other end to the bolt at the edge of the rear bumper and jumped off the slow lumbering truck. As my back hit the tarmac, the friction against the ground started heating my back sending a searing pain through my body.

The truck slowed down even more as our driver knew he was dragging me at the back. Keeping my head away from the ground while being dragged was the hardest to do but I kept my head up and looked at Mohammed, the latter looking pensively at me, no doubt wondering if this distraction could work.

'Dur! Dur!' The guards at the check post ordered us to stop about a hundred metres away. It was nearly 8 am here and men from the neighbouring villages and children were on the road. We caught their attention as it appeared to them that a Turkish army truck were bringing a dead 'enemy' soldier tied at the back, dragging a 'trophy' at their gates. For a few minutes we just waited, checking to see the reaction of the Turkish guards.

To my dismay, we had attracted civilian attention and instead of instinctively sensing danger and leaving the lanes they started converging at our truck. I had to act before the curious civilian crowd came closer to examine the 'dragged enemy'.

'Now Mohammed! The control centres! Fire!'

Ahmed pulled out his M16, firing sharp rounds at the two control centres instantly killing the four men within them. As the other four fired back, our driver and Mohammed ducked back. However, they were no match for Ahmed and Salman's group firing from their long range rifles on the flanks instantly disabling the check point. I fired at the main communication lines coming off the control centres, ensuring no possible calls for assistance to the town's army HQ. It would take a while before the villagers themselves informed them, but I quickly got back into the truck as it speeded towards the gates with Mohammed firing at the bolts to drop the gates on the ground.

We went through keeping a speed of up to forty miles an hour before we found Salman and Ahmed and their men close to the border walls as they climbed over them. We made it past the border and no one expected us to. The only reason we succeeded was because we had just two men coming in from the border. Less strength in less numbers. That always plays into a soldier's mind and they let their guard down. Sadly we could not collect their weapons as we made haste through the border to avoid being seen or studied by the civilians we did not expect at the border. Our truck was probably marked by the civilians and we would need to abandon it to get further towards Kilis.

A treacherous draw but a fateful hand at the gates now brought us close to our mission. However, it would have to mean abandoning the truck and finding another way to get to Kilis. This was not exactly part of the plan, we had anticipated this and were prepared to proceed forward without one.

Looking at each other we smiled. For the moment were alive, fighting the good fight as we believed, not all hope was lost yet as we drove a few more miles before abandoning our truck. Mohammed nodded in appreciation too and I finally felt accepted by my comrades from A'zaz. Little did we know what was in store for us ahead on our way to Kilis but I let that thought slide for the moment as we made our way deep into Kilis.

033 - Approach to Rawanda Kalesi

Having blown right through the Turkish border, we had little doubt the Turks would send planes to survey the entire region from the air. We needed to get off the D850 motorway to avoid getting detected which meant at some point we would need to go through the remote suburb of Akçabağlar.

'How long do we have before we need to abandon the truck, Mohammed?'

Mohammed had been in border incursions into Kilis before, when the Turkish government still supported the Free Syria Army. He had known his way around this region without getting detected but with as many men in this mission, detection would be a challenge unless we split up.

'About thirty minutes so we have to cover as much distance on this truck as we can and go beyond Akçabağlar! Abdullah, drive faster, take the truck up to top speed!'

Mohammed banged on the back of the driver's seat, urging him to speed up. This was dangerous but necessary: a truck with worn out tyres winding up a steep road deeper into Kilis. The truck rumbled unnaturally as we moved faster up the hills as we looked out into the bleak landscape, scouring for snipers, tanks and all forms of enemy warfare. I looked back at the road behind me and found an army convoy jeep following us a mile down, gaining on us. Ahead, Rawanda Kalesi lay just about under 40 miles away putting us in a position of conflict within the reach of our destination. This would be an unwelcome though necessary skirmish with the Turkish forces.

'Do not turn towards Akçabağlar unless we lose them! They have marked us, Abdullah, slow down a little.'

Mohammed pointed to the Turkish convoy jeep following us. We would need to engage them before our move into the suburb and that meant we had to slow down to get them closer.

'The convoy is both bait and a threat for us: we have to get them closer, Abdullah, maintain your speed else we give ourselves away!'

The truck slowed down to about 50 and it seemed plausible as we entered a steep section of the D850. We needed to engage before the slip road towards Akçabağlar came through.

'Naim! Steady the RPG on Salman's shoulder! Everybody get low, lie down! Squat down all of you!'

M16 rifle rounds started whizzing past us as the convoy started firing on us, hitting the trucks metal bonnet at the lower end.

'They are going for the tyres! Salman fire the RPG now!' I had to give the order before Mohammed as the bullets got lower and hit the undertow of the truck. I heard the unmistakeable sound of bullets hitting rubber. The tyres. They got them. Almost in the same instant as Salman fired the RPG, he lost balance and aim as the rear right tyre burst and the truck veered wildly off the highway.

'Hold on to the truck! Abdullah, stop before we turn over!'

Abdullah had not heard us, his fear was compounded when we found the enemy within five hundred yards behind us, shooting at us. He sped faster despite the punctured wheel. The ejected RPG landed just behind the convoy temporarily creating a distance between us and them.

The convoy crew started preparing their sub-machine gun much to our horror and their jeep had slowed down considerably. They wouldn't need to be too close to us: the range of these guns spanned for miles. If they set that machine up, we wouldn't survive.
While they loaded and locked the rounds, Mohammed rallied at Salman.

'Reload the launcher, Salman, fire at the machine gun! Everyone else fire at the men, use your assault rifles! Allah o Akbar!'

The cry to the lord was immediately met with assault rifle fire back from the group of four Turkish soldiers. The fifth one nearly had the machine gun ready. However, this time Salman did not miss: the RPG hit the manned machine gun and the rear of the truck exploded with the men thrown away from the impact. It was over.

'Allah o Akbar!'
We chanted while running towards our enemy, one was still alive, badly wounded bleeding from the spleen. I went up to him,

my rifle pointing downward as pity welled up within me for the wounded soldier,

'Rest, soldier, tell us are there many more behind you?'

Feeling Mohammed's stern gaze I turned around to face him as he ordered, 'Cut up these bastards! Let us make an example of them!'

'We will do no such thing! They are soldiers following orders and so are we. Now, soldier, is there any more coming after you?'

The words had no effect as the arterial bleeding left the soldier lifeless: he had no information to give us as like his dead comrades who were scattered in pieces around the convoy.

Mohammed and I got up and went to convoy truck to assess the damage. A Turkish convoy truck would be our best option to pass undetected through Akçabağlar.

Expecting the worst, however hoping for the best, we popped the engine hood. Much to our relief, the engine was unharmed and the diesel tank was more than half full: enough to get us through the remote suburb and more. Only the question of the battered machine gun and the rear carriage remained.

'Prise the machine gun apart, let's tidy up the truck and bury these bodies as quickly as we can! Turkish authorities know that there has been a breach but what we don't want is them to follow us sniffing up a blood trail! Hurry!'

Mohammed gave the order, looking intently into the horizon should there be more that might follow. He seemed content on me giving the directions to the castle but something in his expressions bothered me as he appeared to be deep in thought. It was not an expression of hate or aggression but that of fear. Were we underestimating our enemy as we approached them?

034 - Fateful Detour

Not everything went to plan at Oncupinar and the encounter with the Turkish convoy had sent our alertness on the razor's edge. We surged onto Akçabağlar with Salman taking over from our injured driver who was visibly shaken but relieved to have made a narrow escape. The poor fellow had caught a bullet in his shoulder when the convoy attacked us. No hospitals in this part of the country, just a few dirty bandages and a stitching needle if available, a disinfectant to prevent the gash from getting worse and last but not the least, Allah's blessing.

Akçabağlar was a small suburb of a few dozen houses, a small market and a few shops selling among other local produce, local Turkish Sim cards. We bought a few from one such shop and discarded our older sim cards from our switched off phones, expecting them to be tracked by now.

'It's Mahmud, he has sent an email while we were entering the border. What is he saying that wily fox, I wonder?'

Mohammed and the others had their own secure email groups that were operated only by the women back in A'zaz to ensure no one could actually trace an email back to the militia. He had just finished downloading an email attachment from Mahmud and looked distressed.

My heart went cold on seeing his stony grave expression, though I didn't have the remotest idea of what Mahmud had written, I was certain the mail did not bode any of us well. Pensively, Mohammed opened the email noting the attachment as we both read it:

'Mohammed my son, Ahmed has been captured by the Syrian army. There is no doubt that the video posted on a propaganda Syrian website is that of him, battered and captured with a clear message sent to those, especially young children, who wish to join us.

He was family and I tried to keep him safe from harm ever since he landed here with us from Timbuktu. A noble soul and well-read too. Naim and he were like brothers watching each other's backs. Please protect him from this message and from what I am about to show you as the Army has made public Naim's entity to the rest of the Arab world.

Ahmed passed in and out of delirium during this painful torture speaking of his uncle Haider and not surprisingly to Naim, unfortunately revealing Naim's origins in the process. Naim is now a much vaunted prize both to the Syrian government and the Americans: both want him dead as he is living proof of the tyranny of both sides.

You must protect him with your dying breath if you have to, Mohammed. The conclusion to our jihad lies in the truth, not just in engaging, killing and driving out our enemies. I hope you will understand what am asking you to do, I hope you will respect it.

Khuda Hafiz,
Mahmud.'

A sense of dread filled me as the attachment revealed a grainy video taken on a phone facing the ground, possibly on one hand as the other seemed to drag a man by the arm. As the video swung back and forth over the ground, we couldn't help noticing that the dragged man's bones below the shins had been broken. So much so that the legs bent horribly in the wrong direction as he was dragged over the gravel and dirt into what seemed to be a camp.

The camera was now set on a table facing the hostage as he was propped onto a chair. My heart sank as I recognised the battered face of my friend: it was Ahmed. He was in much pain with both his legs rendered useless, much so that his captors did not deem necessary to torture him as they started their interrogation.

'Ahmed, tell us about Naim, your comrade: where is he? Why didn't we find him when you were caught? Where is he now? We know everything about you, Ahmed: who you are, where you come from, where you belong. In most of the assaults, the ambush on our army, you and your comrade have been familiar faces. We were there when you and Naim fought us off to protect the lieutenant for the map. Such co-ordinated efforts gain my respect though you will be martyred in your own way, disgraced in ours. Where is Naim, Ahmed? We won't disgrace you for the Sunni bitch that you are, trust me.'

Tears rolled my eyes as I heard myself speak through Ahmed, uttering a prayer of forgiveness for his tormentors.

'Naim--I have spent days looking for him, turned out to be a kaffer for he was never a true soldier of Allah yet he fought like one of us, for us.'

'I know of Naim's true identity for a while now, Ahmed. Tell me what does he seek? What's he after in our land? Why is he here?'

The general's questions had little effect of eliciting a coherent response from my friend suffering immensely from the inflicted pain.

Ahmed seemed to break into a delirious state and apparently speaking to me said, 'Naim, why did you lie to me about your family? Why didn't you wait for me? We could find your family together, meet your son, tell them what a lying ass you have been! How many times uncle Ahmed managed to save your daddy's life, how many times I switched your dad's boots for mine as they were more comfortable having personally gifted by Mahmud!'

'What is he blubbering about?'
The group around him started to whisper.

'Silence, he is half dead already, just talking to the shadows. But it is true what he speaks. Ahmed, what family of Naim are you referring to? Whose son are you referring to?'

Ahmed started to speak, but his trembling lips managed just to utter, 'Uncle, Uncle Haider? I gave up my studies and joined the militia because you never came back. I was alone, slowly everything was finished in that wretched empty house of yours. Akachi, you demon! Lead me to where you dumped my uncle, you infidel. Allah, who am I to fight except

170

myself? Naim, cover for me, we will blow these infidels away in Kilis!'

'He thinks he is fighting a war in Kilis, the lunatic! The whole bunch from Mahmud's clan are crazy! Let's make an example of him as the others!'

There were a few scattered laughs in the background.

'Silence! Ahmed, why Kilis?'

Ahmed smiled at the leader and the video cut short, the next shot showing an army soldier reading out Ahmed's 'crimes against the state'. Almost as soon as sentence was read out, a soldier held Ahmed's head firmly as another promptly beheaded him to the chants of 'Allah o Akbar!' of the rest of the soldiers. The decapitated body on the chair bled to the ground as the soldiers looked on, the camera focused on the dismembered head.

Ahmed looked peaceful now, as if in another painless world far far away from the madness here. His lips quivered as if whispering words no one could hear or listen, then slowly stopped twitching. One would mistake him to be asleep except for his head which was already dismembered from his body. Rage consumed my heart as it burnt a little darker and turned black with the thought of the impending revenge I was planning for these infidels. I will find them and I haven't even decided what I would do to them except for the fact that I would take my time.

Mohammad read the visceral expression of hate on my face and advised with caution.

'We might expect quite a welcome in Kilis, Naim. Get some rest, we have a lot to look ahead when we leave tomorrow morning. Let us pray for Ahmed together now, Naim. A brave man such as him will always be in my prayers.'

'He would prefer to being called 'learned' over 'brave', that priceless fool. I left him alone and vulnerable when I had no choice while he risked his life every time to save mine. Good bye, dearest brother, for I will avenge your untimely end.'

Mohammad looked at me with concern but being a man of strong disposition stopped short of consoling me. Tougher times lay ahead and we had to keep ourselves strong.
We knelt in the evening together, the time for prayer had come.
The time for justice can wait until tomorrow.

035 - The devil's knight in Salem

Having seen the conclusion of Ahmed's life at the hands of the army general had blighted a light within me that I had stubbornly kept alive in the hope of a brotherly reconciliation all this time. I could not expel the image of his dismembered head from my mind as they placed it backward on his decapitated body tied up against a fence. The children played around his body oblivious of the true nature of this act.

I could not sleep, a voice inside told me I was responsible for his death and that I had killed him by not being there to back him up.

'His name is Salem, Naim. I know this general and he fights for nothing except glory in battle. Having encountered him twice before, I barely made a retreat with most of my men slain by him. Salem does not fight with rage or hatred but he is as peaceful as a butcher about his work. If we end up meeting him in Kilis, I am afraid it is the end for you.'

'Ahmed died because I betrayed him, even my biggest sacrifice would not be quite enough to set that wrong right. We had taken many missions together where brave men fell like flies around us either due to inexperience or destiny but we never felt any danger having always protected the other when it mattered.

If we met Salem at Kilis, I will deal with the general, not you

Mohammed. As Mahmud said, you are here to help me but do not become a martyr in my selfish mission!'

I looked at Mohammed, hoping he would understand what I was trying to imply. Mohammed hadn't slept much either, his eyes were bloodshot but from his eyes I could surmise he hoped we would survive through this mission.

'Salem once captured a rebel general of the Free Syrian Army after a long protracted battle on the outer reaches of Damascus. This rebel general survived only to tell the tale Salem had set him out to narrate to us when he recovered him from a dusty back road of the city.
Apparently Salem had not anticipated his capture and there was no schedule for a proper public execution of the rebel and so he improvised: He cut off his trigger finger so he may not shoot an army soldier again, cauterized the wound; blinded his right eye to ensure he could never peek into his sniper rifle view finder ever again and amputated his right leg just to make sure he wouldn't make haste to escape from the approaching army ever again. We are dealing with someone far more dangerous than you have ever met.

Naim, I have a plan but you might have to pay a sacrifice. You could lose your life but it is the only one way we might succeed in rescuing the hostages with the limited ammunition we have.'

As Mohammed shared his plan it was evident that the pivotal moment in my life was near. I had reached a cross road where my actions up to this point would weigh against the fate of my plan to rescue Omar and Sara.

As we approached Rawanda Kalesi, our group left us five miles

174

away from the castle to turn back to Üçpınar. Too much was at risk to allow our finest fighters get under the cross-hairs of the snipers up in the castle. Rawanda Kalesi is a majestic castle on top of a hill and advancing towards it without being detected was impossible. I got off the truck and looked back at my comrades who had been with me this far. It seemed they were certain that I would be slaughtered before I could even meet whom I came for.

'Naim, remember you are not going there as a soldier but as a broken family man. Go in peace without any weapons, remember they cannot kill you as the world now knows about you. You are their weakness and their leverage. They won't kill you yet, but they will do everything else to extract information. Have faith in Allah and may his hand caress your head in the deepest darkest depths of pain though I do wish you well! We will meet on this very road, dear friend, Khuda Hafiz!'

Mohammed's eyes had hope as he bade me farewell then asked the truck to be turned back to Üçpınar. I was alone on the track to Ravanda castle, the imposing ruin looked at me from the hill on which it lay watchful of all those approaching it. The beautiful ruins tempted me to run towards it but I did not, I could not. They were locked in there somewhere, Omar and Sara. Would Sara recognise me? Would Omar honour me as my father? Ahmed, if you are up there, can you see them? Are they alive and well?

A sniper shot, right in front of me broke me away from my thoughts. My mind had drifted in anticipation of this day, so much so I had completely missed observing an approaching truck about a mile ahead of me. I raised my hands and just stood there, waiting. I had been waiting for this day for so long.

175

The truck stopped a few yards away from me and one man got off, he motioned with his raised hand to his men not to fire. Halfway through, he stopped and seemed to recognise me then burst out laughing.

'Naim! It is Naim, my comrades!' he kept up an odd gait, half comic. His comrades joined in laughing.

'Naim! Naim! Naim! The whole world is afire with your name, yet your name is Len...Len, gentlemen!'

Again the group burst out laughing.

'How many lives did you die just to get here? So far into 'enemy' territory?'

Salem could not contain his laughter, neither could his team at the intended pun. We were on Turkish soil and yet Salem had the upper hand on the castle. It was inexplicable.

'Salem, I come here for my family.' No sooner had I said this he knocked a pistol's butt straight on my forehead.

'It is easier to call this infidel Naim, right comrades? Now, Naim, I can read that question on your eyes: is your family alive and well? Come on, ask me.'

As I fell unconscious I heard him say one last thing before I passed out.

'I know you didn't make it this far alone and you will tell me who helped you even if I have to pull that tongue free of you.

Tomorrow we take you back to base, back to our good president who will decide what to do with you, eventually. But today is your lucky day, Naim: You are mine, my only one just for today!'

His laughter died in my ears as I lost consciousness.

'Relax, Naim. Take your time and rest: the answers are coming!'

036 - The lesson of Omar and Sara

'I wondered when you would come here and when you would be here what would we think, Naim? When I say we, I think you know I mean: me, your wife, your son-- all three of us.'

Salem's voice drifted in and out of my head as I was steadily dragged up the broken stone staircase up the castle in the morning sun. His words shook up a part of me and worried me in my dazed state due to the heat and the exhaustion.

'We thought you would come back for us soon after my comrades took your family from Qatmah. Your wife, Sara: she would frequently talk to herself praying for your return, I have overheard it so many times myself.

We knew you had a bit of a reputation working under that infidel dog, Mahmud; so were worried that you would catch up with us guns blazing for your wife and son! Even your son, the wonderful boy that he is, he grew up hoping every day that you would return one day for him. Him whose face he had never seen but knew from his mother's tears.

I saw all that, Naim, and I wondered and waited for your return as I took command of the hostages. Waited for Naim, or rather

'Len' as you were once before you landed in those cursed oilfields!

Your legend is larger than you, Len! When we came to know of your transformation from 'Len' to 'Naim' from the West, we had nothing but awe for you and so we waited!'

'Omar? Sara? Where are they? Salem, I haven't come here to fight, you can see I am unarmed. I came to meet them whom I have been dreaming about for all these years!'

'Five years, Naim! Five! When the hostages were my responsibility three months after the siege at Qatmah, Sara spoke about nothing but of your return. We had to restrain her but had pity on account of baby Omar whose cries we could not suppress. Such is the nature of this conflict: we go to fight a pointless war leaving our families behind, grieving, desolate and without hope; it does bring out the soldier in us, does it not?

All that pain, all that suffering: you see enough of it to a point where it doesn't matter anymore. What matters is ammunition checks, body counts, recon missions and the odd skirmish. Soon all that matters is the conflict, making one feel alive. You felt like that for five years, didn't you, Naim? Is it not why it took you five years to get here while hope and faith receded into your family's minds every single passing day?'

Salem's words, they were a metaphorical whiplash striking me from within bringing involuntary tears to my eyes. Not out of compulsion but by choice, I felt like a pawn in this conflict for the first time since that life changing event back at the oilfields. I hated myself, wretched creature that I was to have come this late. What choice did I have? Mahmud had use of me, I needed his help to recover after what happened at Qatmah but Salem was right: why did it take me this long? Was it possible for me to have come earlier and stand a chance to save my family? 'God, please tell me if I could come earlier and rescue them without a single casualty? Was it possible?'

Salem heard me and replied out loud,'Naim, do not torment yourself and please do not allow me to torment you! While we were coming up the castle steps, I had sent word to your wife and son that you are finally here! They will be up here from the nearby village anytime.

You see, I have helped them settle here to help them forget their families, their past and live a new future. I am a very nice man that way, I gave them hope and a new life. So engrossed have they become in being part of the village folk that am interested what to make of your appearance after all these years! They will be surprised, no doubt, but most importantly, Naim, my dear friend, will they be happy to see you? Let us find out!!'

My heart filled with bitterness as I realised what Salem had done was nothing less than corrupting my family although he could have done worse.

'You did this to ensure those they had left would feel more pain, having lost their loved ones for so long! You are not a saviour, Salem, you are the son of the devil!!'

Salem did not care for my insinuation and announced as a veiled woman, whom I recognised and a fair boy of five or six years old came up the stairs looking steadfastly at me.

'They are here! Sara, fear not the gaze of my men, lift your veil and behold your husband, gone for five years! Naim Nasser!! Or Len Berkowicz, which name would you prefer?'

Here they were, my reason for my existence, all the thousand deaths I had managed to avoid because I survived with the sole determination to save them and bring them home one day. Here they were standing before me. For a moment, I felt time had stopped and I could not breathe, my legs gave away and I fell to the ground. They looked so healthy, no signs of torture, no signs of injury. They were safe, they were fine. I had never actually hope to see them alive, my rage for revenge had kept me alive, not hope. Such was the fine distinction in my motivation to make it this far. Salem was right, though I would not admit it, by reason or partly by choice, maybe I had chosen to take my time to come back for them.

Maybe I wasn't a good father and a good husband after all.

037 – Purgatory

'Behold your father, Omar! The one whom you have been looking for over your shoulder every morning. The one whom you have been praying for every night. The one whom you grew up without all these years, whom your mother awaited with love, hoping he would return!'

Salem's eyes slowly shifted between my son and me, gauging my every response to this gentle petulant boy. Omar was every inch a young Len Bercowicz himself, so it seemed unusual to me that not only did my younger self hated me but would hurt me if given the chance, it seemed like I was self-harming myself.

'The one whom I waited for to ask him why he didn't come back for us, Salem. My mother's tears in vain as we grew with him. Naim, as he calls himself, is not my father, I don't have a father but I do have a teacher, an 'ab rruhi' (God father) in you. This man here means nothing to me or my mother.'

Sara looked on as Omar spoke for himself and his mother. Looking at me, I could see a faint memory of the woman I knew and loved. Much time had passed and I was not with her for the years when she would have needed me the most while Omar grew up from baby to the boy he was now. I had failed them and I was too late in coming back for them. Had war and violence consumed me so much and could I have rescued them earlier? No, not without putting their and my own life at risk, I just did not have the strength or the influence as a common villager of Qatmah to go after the army alone.

A slight twinge in my heart gave my legs further away as I collapsed on the ground in front of them. It didn't matter anymore whether I had failed my family because I didn't come back for them all these years, or they had failed me for not trusting them enough. It was over, it seemed: the purpose to live, the plan and resolve to come back for them. All seemed vain.

'Such admiration, boy! It is the only reason why of all the boys in the village you are the only one allowed to call me by my name. Now, punishment, my boy, that is what we have to decide for this man here! Look at him, he has already collapsed on the ground out of fear. Tie him up!'

Salem's soldiers tied me up against a pillar, hands to the side.

'Now we know, boy, your father here is wanted by our western allies alive. So we cannot behead him in a pit and purify him as you would have wanted. We can however punish him in ways that can keep him alive before we hand him out tomorrow morning. Take my sword, boy.'

Salem handed what appeared to be a ceremonial family heirloom of a sword to the diminutive boy.

'It is light, is it not, Omar? Belonged to my great grandfather and still used to purify liars and blasphemers! I want you to chop off your father's hand above the left wrist. Do it quickly then we will cauterize the veins to stop the bleeding. Would that be enough, Omar?'

'Not quite enough, Salem, but it will do. But tell me why should I do it to this man?'

To my horror, I realised Omar had been radicalised to the point of hurting his own family by the orders of the one man who provided for him all these years. From Sara's indifferent gaze turned to the Sara I knew and loved as she attempted to stop Omar.

'Salem, it is too harsh a sentence on him. You have protected and fed us but my son is too young to be earning his place in your army yet! Could we not wait to think what we should do?'

'No, we cannot. It is getting late, time is running out before this infidel is taken back to the western camp. We have time for just one lesson, one example to be made of this impostor, a traitor to our nation and cause! Your husband is nothing but a mercenary to suit his selfish needs and this is the punishment! He will live but without his family and without a hand'

You are learning well, Omar! You might join me sooner on Allah's cause than you think! Ok, get on with it! Take his left hand off!'

As Omar came closer to me, I did not feel fear of the pain from what was about to happen. I could see him closely now, he looked like me when I of the same age. It felt as if this moment had split into two timelines, showing myself as a boy and a man, the same person facing each other. We were the same though born in different circumstances thus showing two very different sides of the same man undertaking an act of self-harm.

The blade was sharp as I felt Omar's blow cut through my hand, he didn't quite make it all the way through being a boy but like his father he had strong hands, ensuring the second blow freed the severed hand from my body. I cannot explain what I felt through my body as the pain made me cry out and soon I fell into a daze, only remembering in flashes to hear Sara weep.

'Allah and all the Gods to whom I could pray had I known their names: will you have mercy upon me and separate the pain I feel from my body? Within my being my soul struggled against the cage of my body as I pleaded to have me taken away in the face of the searing pain I felt from the dismembered hand.

'I love both of you so much, I have missed you growing up, Omar. I would have come earlier if I could but I wouldn't let that happen again--'

This was the last I said before I passed out.

'Naim, are you awake? Have some water, here.'

I heard her voice as I woke up to find myself laid out on the rocky floor of the castle entrance. It was Sara, Omar was sitting by her side.

'Sara, Omar, I wanted to get hear earlier but I couldn't. No ordinary man could just come after the army and not get killed. I needed Mahmud's help to get to A'zaz where I thought you would be. Is Salem around?'

'No, he has gone to the village to hire new recruits. Omar rides with him tomorrow, to see you sent off to the western camp. Naim, this waiting, all this longing, this was in vain! I thought you had died, Omar missed you so badly that there were nights when he would not stop crying! Salem came to know of our story, very soon he came to know who you really were. Omar is but a prize for him: a victory proclaiming even a son of the West can be radicalised to fight the holy war! This is the reason why he is nice to us and provides special attention and training to him.'

'Mama, we shouldn't speak so much to this man, he is going back tomorrow, back to where he came from. He never came for us, mother, he abandoned us just long enough so that would either learn to survive on our own or die! Let us go back to the village, it is getting late.'

'Omar, you are my son! I do not expect you to forgive me but every day of these last few years you and your mother have been in my thoughts, thinking about the ways to get to you, to rescue you.

Sara, did you notice Omar looks like me, you remember my childhood pictures, he is me!'

Sara cried as Omar tried to take her away but not before she rebuked him.

'Omar, he is your father, all this while you wanted to meet him now that he is alive, you want to run away. No father has made it this far and yet here he is, son. For what you did, which is inexcusable we can at least wait longer?'

186

Sara took my head on her lap and looked at me. There she was, the Sara I knew, looking at me, her head against a backdrop of stars. I didn't feel my pain at all for the time being. We have been like this before, in another place, another time and all I felt despite the searing pain in my hand was bliss.

I slowly passed away into sleep in the warm comfort of her being, for the moment, I felt safe and loved, even nurtured in her cradle.

038 - Muted Twilight

Heart, slow down if time would not: I was unwilling to let go of these moments as if they were cherished marbles in my hand stolen from the shop window. My family was safe and they were here with me. It felt surreal, almost as if we were united in heaven long after we would have died.

I passed in and out of consciousness as the feeling of bitter relief engulfed me. I felt free and complete if only for those fleeting moments had stayed longer with me. Five long years had passed, my hope and my will to re-unite with Omar and Sara had waxed and waned over time but here I was with them finally but in strange and difficult circumstances.

'In my mind I had buried you, Naim. Did you believe we were still alive after all these years? I can barely recognise you but I fail to find my husband behind the harshness of your face. You have become one of them, you must have. What did you have to do to come this far? Having witnessed the be-headings of many fathers and sons in the villages we stormed by, I had made peace with God that you may have passed on to the other side.'

I heard Sara speak as I opened my eyes to notice that bleeding stub of my right hand had been cauterized and bandaged into a swelling bundle. It did not hurt as badly any more, just a twinge compared to the comforting site of my family.

'Am not sure if I am happy or sad to finally see you after giving you up for good. So much has happened since you weren't there for us. Saleem provided for both of us where others would have given us up to the desert if they could. What were the odds for us to meet after not having heard from you for years?

After we were taken at Qatmah, we were used several times as human shields on our long journey to this village. Omar was a baby, yet the army took mercy on him and fed us both though they have killed the older boys that were taken with us. He could have caught a disease or died in circumstances where no baby could have survived, but he did survive. Yet he didn't because of Saleem who is the saviour, the hero in your son's eyes.

To be finally able to see you today though I hoped he would run to you instead Salem's hold on his young heart has not waned. We came a long way in Qatmah, didn't we? We had blended in with love and respect for the local community, worked for the same community and lent a helping hand to all those who needed it. Omar was to be our example in the face of these challenges, a desert rose proudly thriving in the heat, unlike others who would wilt in the harshness that surrounded us. Why did God choose to test us, what did we do wrong?'

'Sara, do you remember asking Him why he gave us happiness when we were happy? Why do we ask Him only when we undergo pain and suffering? I have done nothing noble in choosing a side in the worst civil war of this century but I chose only to find you, find Omar and if I could, find Him.

I never always believed you were alive and I had nightmares of Omar dying out in the bleak desert but I had to know. The question kept me alive, this urge to search kept me running, trying to find out what God had kept in store for me.'

I felt quite weak and raised a faltering eye to my son, beckoning him closer.

'Omar, I have failed you. You deserve better but I love you my son, even if it meant death by your hand. You respect Salem for what he has done for you, for your mother and you should.

For whatever reason he kept you and your mother alive so that we could meet today even if we have met under these circumstances, I am grateful to him. But you don't see that men like him are the very reason why we are here today? Sara, did you ever tell him?'

Sara shook her head. Omar had grown up all these years yet he was still young. She was still the Sara I knew, the storm in her being never apparent on her face which was as calm as still water.

'We would never see you again and we had been provided for by Salem. Why would I risk my life and our son's by filling his head with the truth when a simple lie would help him survive and live?'

Omar had not fully comprehended how Salem's orders had such a hold on him but he seemed to have realised the terrible mistake he had made.

'Father, I was told that you were a kaffer, a coward to have left a mother and a baby child all these years. I have been listening to several of his 'little words of wisdom' he gave to the villagers here. This is 'jihad' not just against the blasphemers, but against

America who are destroying our nation. Salem says such violence must be met with greater violence all in Allah's name. It is all written in the Quran: the great show of violence is in effect a deterrent to the blasphemers to stop them from the grave crimes they commit, for a far bigger judgement awaits them in Allah's court!'

'Omar, although you might think these words come from a rebel who has killed, just listen to this once: I have killed many a soldier on the field, but without passion, without hate, without anger, with a prayer. It is a burden that gets heavier as you go further, my son. Your mother had not told you yet, but we would be in London right now, in a safer place. We would be worrying only about your education, your friends, your swimming lessons. I dreamt so much about you having a normal life than counting dead bodies and fighting this 'holy war'. This is not who you are, Omar, you are better than them or us,'

Yes, you were born here, but your father isn't Naim, the rebel soldier but Len, an engineer helping people to build lives, making lives better rather than destroying them. You were born out of our love and hope that we could get back to our way of living. We wanted you with us, maybe tell you one day of that life changing event that made us change who we were to who we are now. We wanted to prove to the world that love could still blossom in such harsh and bleak conditions.

Sadly, this got worse as men of violence turned our destiny towards being prisoners here. Salem is not your father, Omar. He will train you to be tough, to survive by killing, pillaging and destroying others but it is not Allah's will to live like this and not yours either. It is easier to burn down a house than to build it,

191

easier to kill one who challenges your beliefs than to observe how you can weather his storm with your inner calm!'

Omar was just a five year old boy, I didn't expect him to understand what I was trying to tell him but the boy was wiser than his years.

'I thank Salem for what he did for us, father. We had no hope, mother would cry every night when I pretended to sleep. Even now we have no hope, you see, you will be handed over to the western camp as he said and we will never see you again! Why did you come back to haunt us?'

'No Omar, I am here for you and your mother.'

Sara looked at me, I could see the familiar fondness in her eyes but were welling up with tears.

'Naim, you always gave hope even in the most difficult times. It's one of the qualities of incorrigible hope in you I have always loved. Tomorrow morning I will lose you again when they take you back to the embassy. I know you mean well but don't, for God's sake lie to me to make me feel better. What do you mean that you are here for us?'

'No, I have put the best part of these last five years trying to get to you both. What were the odds of seeing both of you alive in this war? If I lose both of you, I might never find you again. We will be safe from harm tomorrow morning when I am taken to the camp. You will have to put your faith in me. I have come this far and am not letting go easily either.'

Both looked at me asking the unasked question: Why was I here and what would happen tomorrow morning?

192

039 – Ambush

'Tell me more about Ahmed, abi! Why isn't he here with you? Will we ever meet him?'

From my fleeting senses that ebbed within me, in and out of consciousness as exhaustion and a loss of blood brought within me a sense of relief and finality. It seemed Omar was warming up to the thought that he really did have family unlike Salem's harsh reminders.

'What Ahmed would not do to meet you, Omar! He would be so proud to see you strong and healthy born off this war stricken land. There is much to tell, Omar but that will have to wait for another time, when the three of us will be in our home, safe from harm.'

Sara looked at me, unsure of how I would keep such a promise, yet she did not speak again. Her eyes were filled with an emotion she had long forgotten had resided in her, that of relief and love.

Omar and Sara had not left my side all night as we tried catching up on the time we had lost. Ahmed's name kept coming up as Omar listened with rapt attention of the many travails of his departed God father. By early morning I had told them to leave to avoid any suspicion among Salem and his men.

Early dawn, while I lay shivering in the open ruins of the castle, I realised how beautiful it looked in the rising sun.

Ravanda Kurusu was a castle back from the age of the crusaders, a sprawling rampart of ancient stone and mortar. Even the trees around the hill looked as if they were here for centuries.

I had read about this castle when I was back in school as a young boy. Maybe what is taught to us back in high school does prepare us for your future? The irony of my question made me laugh out loud though the pain from my arm kept my laughter in check.

'Have they already left, your family? I told you, Naim, it was already in vain! They are happy here, we have made sure they have been well fed and integrated with the village below. How much pain that infidel Mahmud must feel when he will learn that his daughters are now well settled here and do not miss their father! It is a labour of love, don't you think? Your boy, oh, what do I tell of him? He is the best of the lot, he will do me proud when he becomes a commander fighting those whom you protect! All this is a very win-win situation for me don't you think?

Salem was relishing the fact that my family had not spent the night here with me. To Salem, this meant he had won: families broken apart, mission accomplished for radicalising a boy and hence preparing him to be a war-dog like him. I looked at Salem, giving him the impression that I understood and accepted every word of his.

'So to complete turning Omar full circle, he is to join us. To deliver his own father to the western camp, never to see him again!

Omar, come on over now! Everyone, load up the truck, we are going to the camp.'

I hadn't expected Omar to join the entourage back to the camp: the boy seemed capable but he was my son, not one of Salem's. I looked at Omar and he looked at me uncertainly, I returned his look with a reassurance: It was going to be alright.

We went down the same road toward Kilis, this time a more direct route. Salem had, as expected, chosen his best and elite commanders to come with him. The castle and the village would have to be less guarded today as the package was far precious than the hostages safe in the village.

I was at the back of the truck, looking back at the beautiful castle hoping in my heart that I could come back for Sara when the time came.

'Zzt! Zzt!' Sharp buzzing sounds, the unmistakable bullets of an assault rifle hitting the truck's undertow sharply broke my thoughts.

'We are under fire! Over to your left over the dunes! And keep driving: we are only a mile away from the camp, don't stop!'

The convoy personnel got down in formation into sniper and assault groups, started firing at the direction of the bullets.

I turned around to see Salman and Abdullah taking aim with their RPG launcher about a thousand yards away. Mohammed's plan was starting to unfold, he was moving across the dunes with the other men to flank the truck from the other end.

The truck shuddered as the driver picked up speed along the dusty road, taking the turn towards the camp just a mile away. As it turned on the road, the length of the truck was available as a target. Salman took aim as I heard the RPG release from his launcher.

'Omar! Get down! Flat on the floor and hold on tight!'

Cold sweat ran down my face as I braced for the RPG impact as it made contact with the rear offside wheel with such force that I realised it was a bad idea. Lunging towards Omar I covered him in my arms, shielding him from the heat of the explosion under the truck.
The truck lurched upwards as the blast imploded under the truck. As it fell back on the ground, it turned, twisted and overturned as the rear wheels were jammed from the blast.

Omar cried out but I had him covered with my arms with my back to the floor as the truck overturned. For a moment, I felt love and peace in this horrid moment of the violence around us. Omar, my little boy, he appeared hard and unmoved in the castle yet here he was soft and lovely in my arms, my own flesh and blood. Five years I hadn't held him and I wasn't about to let him go, he is mine.

'Form a circle around Naim, quickly! Omar! You betraying infidel come off that man at once! Come here before I decide to lash you tonight, you traitor!'

Salem's eyes were thick with rage as he saw Omar in my arms. He would certainly kill the boy if he got hold of him. Despite my cauterized arm I held on to the shaking boy refusing to take

Salem's orders. I felt Omar's trousers go a warm wet as he held on to me tightly, refusing to let go.

'Let him be, Salem! He is my boy, he is with me now. Don't, for the love of Allah, do anything wrong! You have kept him safe from harm all these years for which I will be forever grateful but do not take away my son from me. Think, Salem before you act. He respects you, loves you for what you have given him up to this day. But he is family, my family. Omar is just a young boy, have mercy on him and let him be with me!'

Salem's eyes filled with emotion and while I did not expect it, tears were flowing down his eyes.

'Omar, you fool, you lying dog! I raised you as my own when I should have killed you! I won't hurt you, come back to me! We will get to fight these infidels together, in glory of Allah! Come here, Omar, I order you!'

'Omar's path is not of violence anymore, Salem! He is coming with me and he will leave this war and its violence far behind! By Allah's grace he will read and study instead of holding a gun and go to war with you killing people! Let us go, I ask you, let us leave!'

I realised Salem loved Omar in his own way, raising him to be like him: he was not Omar's father but he treated him like a son who would follow in his footsteps. There was no reasoning with this man as this was a fight between two fathers.

Salem drew his rifle, taking aim at me when a stray bullet got his ribs from the side and he slumped backward. Suddenly an unexpected group of rebels emerged from the direction of the shot: It was Mahmud Nasser!

'Omar! Untie my hands we need to get out of here now!' I cried to Omar, who was clearly not prepared for the intense ambush unfolding before his very eyes. The truck's fuselage had caught fire, we had only moments before getting off the truck.

Omar picked Salem's rifle and shot the unsuspecting soldiers who were engaging with the rebels. It had to be done.
He haltingly aimed at Salem.

'No Omar, don't kill him, son. Don't do this, he will be judged in Allah's court, not here!'

Salem was dying, the bullet had started to bleed him profusely. Looking at me he said just one last thing which I would never forget.

'Omar, I love you as my son though I am not your father. If the war made me brutal and ruthless towards men, women and children, I always felt I had to be gentle to you. Your little fingers on my beard had to remain unharmed, my son. You will grow up to be a fine soldier one day, far better than me. You are mine, always be. Who are governments and leaders or a father to tell me otherwise?'

Omar lowered the gun, both of us looked at Salem as he looked at us and breathed his last.

We ran away towards Mohammed and his men, though we could not help but look at the 50 odd men with Mahmud who quickly overpowered the remaining entourage in a matter of minutes.

'Sire, you are here! Your daughters and my wife are in the village, let us get them. I am so glad to see you here! Please meet my son, Omar!'

'Why are you dressed as a kaffer, boy? Someone give him our clothes! Come on boy, we will take you to the embassy, Abdullah will take you there. Naim, you are coming with us to the village to get our womenfolk back! I could not miss this for the world, I am old now and I rather see my daughters once before I die! Come on, let us go back to the village.'

Mohammed greeted me with a wry smile.

'You lived after all', looking at my bloodied hand he continued, 'a small price, my friend. Mahmud, we must take Naim to a doctor once we have rescued the remaining women and children. He is still bleeding!'

'I am fine, Mohammed. Seeing you and Mahmud and our men together, I have never felt better!'

It was true, I felt hopeful: for the first time in all these years, it seemed destiny was helping set everything right again. For Sara, for family, for all those who lost theirs several years ago; we proceeded for one last assault.

040 – Rescue

Sara had been filling water from the local wells of the Gökmusa Village in preparation for the men, her captors, to come back after Naim's handover to the western camp. Five of Salem's men were left behind to keep a close eye on the erstwhile hostages who were co-habiting with the villagers now.

While these men were not the best of Salem's warriors, they were the meanest of the lot and took particular pleasure in inflicting pain to those who still resisted naturalisation in these quarters. But not today, they were on the backfoot as Sara noticed.

'They must have known of his escape by now.'
Sara thought as she assembled her pots of water, taking them back to the castle. Her heart was pounding as she took the stairs up the castle: did Naim escape from Salem and the western camp and save Omar? Are they coming back for her? Sara knew that Naim would come back for her but right now she felt dazed and confused.

It had been years since she always thought of Naim and Len as two distinct beings: the one after and before the change to their lives. She had always given the way to Len's ambition even if it meant leaving the country for a while. Even if it did mean, in the absence of a certain future and changed identities they had decided to conceive Omar because they loved each other. Len was however, the city yuppie whom she fell in love with but Naim she had come to love and respect: he was the darker version of Len who could kill to get to his family by whatever means necessary.

However, comparisons between Len and Naim always brought the comparison back to herself: the Sara of 'then', before the attack at the Golan Heights oilfields and the Sara of 'now': Earlier she too was the city yuppie who would be present in every protest against the free will of the people.
But this was a bit of a contradiction to the Sara of 'now' for she wouldn't consider such a public stand, in which case motherhood and her love for Naim had changed everything to the painless detachment she felt at the prospect of being rescued. At times she did feel a part of her taken away when she agreed to come to the Golan Heights exploration area with Len, then again when she agreed to have a baby at Qatmah despite the fact of what had happened at the oilfields. Naim had been gone for a long while, nearly five years and she felt more of the Sara of today, of 'now' than ever before.

Unfortunately, when one says that one nation's terrorist is another nation's freedom fighter, the views are often a paradox in relation to each other. The burqa was more comforting to her psyche than the thought of going back to the western world and get back to living the way she did. It seemed impossible.

At least that is what I thought when I came guns blazing into the quiet village of Gökmusa with Mahmud.

'There they are! Kill those infidels and burn them!'

Mahmud motioned towards the five men who were attempting

to imprison Sara and a few of the women who ran towards Mahmud, they were his daughters.

'My daughters Nazneen, Farhian and Naseem! Come here, it's me, your father!'

Tears of joy welled up from both sides as they met up and embraced like two sides of the river long blocked by a dam now broken. It was pure simple relief and love to see Mahmud reunite with his daughters.

'Sara! It is ok, we can now finally escape! Mahmud is here to help us, we are finally here to get back as we always wanted!'

My words seem to follow hollow upon Sara as she did not run towards me as I had expected. She stayed where she stood, confused and as broken as a dove with injured wings.

'What is the matter, Sara? We do not have much time! Omar is already in safe hands, we must leave now!'

'I can't leave with you, Len. Not this time. I have to stay back.'

The words went as a dagger through my heart. The thought of Sara changing had always haunted me. After all that I had put her through, it would come as no surprise that Sara who was familiar to being independent in the west would have to find a way to adapt as she did in Qatmah to be able to survive. In this regard, we were exactly identical.

'Sara? We are going back home where a safe future awaits us Back in London. Omar is already in the camp waiting for us, this is real, Sara! This is it, we will start anew, renew our vows with our Omar in a place safe from harm! Let us leave before the Turkish forces storm the village!'

'Naim! My son, don't you see it by your own eyes! How can you miss seeing that she is with child?'

At that moment, Salem's last words before he died echoed in my mind. The unthinkable sprung to my mind.

'Uncle Naim, please forgive Sara: she was forced into joining Salem in the camps. Had she not complied they would have killed Sara and Omar at once. This is not her fault.'

Mahmud's daughters with bent heads told me the shocking truth: Sara was in no condition to run or make this journey in this condition.

'Naim! I am sorry, you have to go alone this time. All these years I have been trying to think in my mind how I would tell you about the choices I made so that our son and I could live. If I try to escape by foot or otherwise, it would be an act of murder for the child in my womb!'

Mahmud came over to me, 'Naim, leave this matter to me. You cannot take her with you at this time, you have to come back and I do not know how. If she travels in this state, her baby could die and so could she. You have to trust me after all that we have done for each other. Do not try to risk this!'

It was impossible not to feel the helpless rage I felt at the moment, despite which I cried standing five feet away from Sara. Though she loved me she was afraid of me and would not comfort me. The whole point of waiting for years before gaining enough powers to get to this rescue seemed pointless.

'No. How could I never see this happening? All these years spent in the pursuit of your rescue when I have already lost you. Why?'

I could manage no more. We were more than just parents for Omar, we were one before he came into this world. With a heart as black and heavy as coal, I looked at Sara, bent down to take her hand and rest it on my forehead one last time. We had been here before, her hand on my forehead as we sat down on the green parks behind Soho. Almost as if the moment had repeated itself in a different time and space.

'Sara, I did this to you and I am sorry.'

I looked at Mahmud with gratitude, the grizzled old elder looked back. It was the day we both had been waiting for except for a much nuanced conclusion to our rescue efforts. Qatmah's villagers who had naturalised with the local population looked on, some came across to us pleading us to take them back to their families. It was a quiet joyous moment for many while others cried quietly, especially those who had waited, like me, for this day.

'There is a problem. We have a small patrol of Turkish soldiers headed this way. They are already too near, Mahmud, we cannot escape without being shot at!'

Mohammed looked keenly at Mahmud as he gave this message, knowing full well that a defensive retaliation would save lives than a desperate escape.

'How many, Mohammed? How did they know?'

'About fifty of them: the Americans sent them when they got wind of the ambush. I think they are coming to kill you, Naim!'

So I realised: the Western camp wanted a safe return but the ambush showed how little control they had in the desert. No hostages this time, they want to wipe me out with the others in the name of fighting terror.

041 - So long, farewell

'Naim, you are not going anywhere, stay by my side!
Mohammed, get our men to form a perimeter around the village!
No one gets to come in as we hold position and get Salman and
Abdullah on the higher ground with the RPG launchers for
counter strike!'

Mahmud hugged his daughters and bade the villagers to retreat
to their homes. Sara held my hand and pulled me aside, tears
streaming down her face.

'There are five of Salem's men somewhere within this village!
They know your face well and will kill you. Let me stay with you
and they might hesitate knowing it is their commander's child I
carry!'

She had changed in these years, she was steps ahead of me since I
met her yesterday after all these years. We heard heavy trucks in
the distance rolling by the gravel roads alongside the castle when
they stopped, filling the air with an uneasy quiet.

The men quickly made a perimeter formation around the village
taking vantage points from the little windows of the rural houses,
ready to aim and fire.

A huge hiss and a tremendous boom erupted about a 100 meters from us throwing debris, the air blast itself dislodging us from where Sara and I stood. Sara held my hand, pulling me towards a narrow alleyway towards the hill leading to the castle.

I motioned to Mahmud that we were going towards the castle to which he motioned us to come back.

'It's too dangerous! Come back here, son!'

We heard the unmistakeable sound of a drone over the hills, its quiet operation with a hissing sound was a dead giveaway: It was a U.S drone turning towards the main street where we stood sheltered under a small mud packed shelter.

As the men fired at the drone, agile as it was, it was quickly able to turn around taking accurate aim to fire a couple of short range missiles. No survivors, even the children in the houses were charred. The horrific nightmare had just started.

Ahmed was on the tower of the mosque: an aimed RPG hit on the drone landed the wretched aircraft on the ground but not before neutralising him. We watched in horror and anguish as his body slumped from the tower to the ground.

Guns, drones, infantry and a whole murderous garrison had been unleashed upon us to hide an international embarrassment: They are here to eliminate me, all of whom I knew, all of whom I loved.
The drone had already breached our perimeter adding to our misery as the Turkish soldiers made their way in by trucks. Our men shot at the entering trucks neutralising them but there were about ten out of fifteen still moving in the convoy.

'I have to go, Mahmud! I can draw their fire away from you while you retreat safely with those who can leave with you! Sara, stay with Mahmud, stay with his daughters!'

She wouldn't let my hand go: I looked up and for that moment, there she was, the woman I knew and loved. She hugged me for what seemed a frozen eternity. It felt like almost my whole life as Len flashed before my eyes.

'I will come back for you. Go and keep safe, Sara.'

'There is a path the women folk use to deliver water to the castle, let me lead you there. I will come back here once I have seen you leave safely. Keep our Omar safe, Naim. He is me and you. I am your past and present but Omar is our future, live for him!'

She knew, despite the seemingly impossible promise I had just made: I would keep my word. The plan was delicate but I wanted her on my side at this time after all this time. Mahmud handed me enough ammunition, a rifle, grenades to get through to the exit.

'Go in peace, Naim, but come back in peace too, son.'

He kissed my forehead and bade me as they retreated from the east end of the village. We ran out in the open towards the convoy and neutralised the first truck. Soon the bullets rained on me like fire, there was little cover as we ran through the narrow alleys.

At this point, I noticed a few Caucasian mercenaries skim through the alleyways like jackals. The trucks fell quiet within a matter of minutes as these mysterious band of soldiers kept neutralising target after target with amazing stealth and ferocity.

'There he is, kill him!', someone shouted in Arabic. It was Salem's men as they found me heading up the flat lands towards the castle. Shots were fired and one caught my spleen and I fell, Sara cried out to the men to stop.

'No! I can't die! My son needs me! I need to come back for Sara!'

Thoughts clouded my mind as the searing pain of the flesh wound made me dizzy. As I lay down on the dusty ground, realising I was losing blood fast I thought I had never been shot this bad before. I was saved, up until now, for this day, to meet Sara and Omar and ask for their forgiveness.

'Len! Len, oh dear, we need to take you back to the village! We can't lose you, please I__'

I saw Sara's crying face in front of me as she tried to say something but being pulled away from me. They have finally caught up with us and she was being taken away.

'Please, no. Stop, don't you take her away from me!'
The bright sun's rays hit my eyes and I instinctively closed them.

'Thank you, lord, I accept what you have in store for me.'
My last prayer before the world darkened around my eyes.

'Is he alive, mate? That wound looks bad, not good for a clean extraction.'
I opened my eyes, it was one of the Caucasian jackals looking back at me.

'Len, we are the British extraction team sent to extract you. Smile, you are in good hands!'

The British? Wait, what about Sara, please take her with me! My thoughts would not translate to my mouth as I fell into a deep induced sleep. The light faded away to darkness as I felt lifted away in the air as I saw a chopper above my head.

'No, wait! Sara! '

No one responded as the world darkened in front of my eyes, faded to black as I felt my exile had just begun.

042 — The Fallout

'You are but one statement away from losing your job, your credibility and your freedom! Superseding a chain of command to pass confidential dossier minutes to a select member of the executive branch is an act of indiscipline! It is a lack of your trust in the way MI5 works, Sam. You are just about to lose everything you hold dear in your life.'

Intelligence director Lewis looked over on to Sam as he made the consequences of his actions clear: Sam had made a disclosure of the dossier of the city in siege. The dossier had a profile on me, as Sam told me later. The profile had everything they needed to know what I and my family had gone through. Yet they had waited with bated breath to see what would happen next and did nothing.

'Sometimes the best action is to refrain from taking a side in a war that is not ours, Sir. We have learnt our lesson in our participation in conflicts that are not our own and I agree with you on that principle and I would have followed the protocol. But we could not keep the remarkable story of this man under wraps for long, this is no more about nations or their politics. This is the reflection of our politics in the life of this remarkable young man. None of his actions had anything to do with the state of affairs but for his heart to live, survive and defy circumstances out of his control, to protect his family! How can we bury this story of hope and a perfect example of defiance in the face of terror?'

'Even if I did agree with you, our hallowed institution won't and this is why I would be expecting your resignation letter at my desk by tomorrow morning, Sam.
Dave that goes for you as well. As of today, both of you are no more a part of MI5. We will issue a gag order for whatever you wish to disclose to the public. You are dismissed!'

Dave felt embarrassed after being let off in this manner, he had served in the MI5 administrative office slightly longer than Sam. However, he remembered the tea stall owner in India, with whom he had shared many a tea in earthen pots that enhanced the taste of the masala 'chai' even more.

'Am just glad helping the tea maker, Sir.'

Lewis looked at Dave incredulously, wondering if Dave took his termination quite seriously.

'Am sorry? Dave, are you all right?'

'The tea stall owner in India, sir, he would keep the dust at bay from his stall throughout the day. All that dust from the cars on the dusty roads. Just a little water, all it took was a little effort to keep his precious tea he served, he became a part of the wholesome service to his customers. I just helped keep the dust at bay from the very poison of Daesh as I saw fit. Had we not passed your command this remarkable engineer from London would have died an unfair death.
My conscious is clear, Sir. I don't wish to sell a story to the public. If our actions helped save the life of this man, I am

content in this thought. Would I have been able to forgive myself otherwise? I am not sure!'

Lewis paused as he looked at Sam and Dave, exhaled, then stood up.

'Have a good day, gentlemen. Leave your papers and clear out your disclosure forms before you exit the building.'

Sam recounted the brief meeting to me as I awoke at Barts hospital intensive care ward.

'Don't disclose this to anyone, we are not even here, you understand? Len, your son is safe here with your parents. Tough chap, your kid, but he is adapting well to his new home.'

Looking at my face, it had become apparent to Dave that I was oblivious to Sara's fate.

'Our team could not extract Sara, Len. She was taken away back into the village by a group of what appeared to be Syrian soldiers. We know their training and did not risk a pursuit. Besides, you had to be airlifted else with all that blood loss you would have died. This was a covert operation, even the U.S. of A did not have a clue, do you understand?'

Sara's face, the final fleeting moments at the village exit flashed right before my eyes. What would they do to her? Could Mahmud rescue her from Salem's team of vicious killers? I had lost her again, failed again to keep the hope alive that I kindled. I closed my eyes to retain those fleeting moments in my heart and cried involuntary tears.

'Len, you need to rest, the doctor has mentioned you could have Angina and an irregular heart among other physiological ailments. Nurse, does our patient have enough painkillers? He is in pain, could you please tend to him? Len, we have to leave now. Just rest as you recover here, I can't give you all the answers you want. Give it time, you have our numbers: call us if you need any help'

'Thank you, Sam and Dave.' I could not open my eyes to thank them: Sara's image in my mind's eye was so strong that it felt my eyes were open when in fact they were closed.

'Okay. Later then.' Sam motioned to Dave to leave me to recuperate. They turned once more at the door to look at me, then they were gone.

I was counting the days till I could meet Eric, face to face. It would not be a happy coincidence to see me alive, not for him. Joan must know for she and Sara were one at heart. That day to meet was not far, I must recover before it is too late to keep my promise to Sara.

043 - Eric has a plan

'No, that is impossible. We had the report from the Israeli government. This is a nightmare: are you sure it is Len who landed in London? He will be here, he will come for me. Brian, you know what to do. Just let me know when it is done.'

Eric hung up the phone, it was three am: he found it hard to believe that his disastrous plan of sending Len to the ill-fated project was about to destroy his life and reputation. All his career had passed without as much of a negative mention as he played stakes that got higher with time. The heights of his unscrupulous deeds had reached a nadir, it was only going to be downhill from here.

Joan looked at Eric's tortured face but felt no compassion for her husband.

'We have to come clean on this, Eric. Hasn't the guy had enough already? The news last night mentioned Sara was missing though his son has also been rescued. We need to speak to him, ask him for our forgiveness: he was, after all your friend, the only one among the other sharks, Eric. Just think carefully of what you are doing.'

Joan spoke these words carefully, with the faintest hope that Eric might consider her words for once.

'You knew? This is shocking: we should have got this from the oval office instead of the evening news! After what I have done with him, he will never forgive me. He is coming after me. No one is sure how he survived five years in the mouth of this madness but he has, God!'

'Eric, Len and Sara were family and God parents to Josh, have you forgotten? It wasn't until after they went missing did I realise that you had sent them to slaughter on the odd chance that the exploration might satisfy Innofuel's greed for oil. The poor man is short of a limb: apparently some Syrian soldiers wished to make an example of him. Let him forgive you or I will not be able to forgive you this time!'

Eric's silence answered Joan, who recoiled in disgust. She got off the bed and walked over to the windows looking at the darkened skies where the morning sunshine had not yet come through.

'Joan, he will destroy us. You know what it took to get this far up at InnoFuel, don't go all moral and high minded on me now.'

'I gave up that job because I couldn't live with the lies anymore, Eric. I thought keeping my distance would help reduce the guilt I felt in the manner we have dealt with the oil demand from the Middle East. I couldn't survive in that sea of lies and greed in the hope that Josh would grow up being fairer to the world than you and I have been!'

'It's 4 am in the morning, so am going to assume that's your hangover from last night's party talking, Joan. Go back to sleep.'

'If you attempt to harm Len, I will give up on you, Eric! This is but a lose - lose situation for you. Have it your way.'

Joan left the room and went to Josh's bedroom, hoping to have some solace from holding on to her son. Her's not Eric's : she had resolved not to let Eric's ruthless nature inherit Josh's young heart.

Eric knew Joan far too well to know that she meant every word she said. This was his survival now, the thought of losing all that he had accumulated over these years, wealth and power, was too much to bear.

He dialled into the Oval Office operative hesitantly.

'Operator. Mr Eric Leighton I presume?'

'Yes, it is me. As you aware, a ghost is back to haunt us. There is however, another cause of concern in relation to the recent events.'

'We are aware. What do you want us to do about it?'

'What? I mean, h-how do you know? I mean, is my home bugged?'

Eric felt uncomfortable in the thought that the syndicate had ears in his own house. Was his ascension to the higher echelons within Innofuel not enough to guarantee some privacy?

'Do you have to ask, Eric? Now please tell me what is bothering you in relation to this ghost? This line is encrypted and secure.'

Eric sat down at the edge of his bed, as he weighed down the implications of what he was to request for. The implications were significant, the consequences were dire, but it had to be done. Only he could give the order, only he could allow this to happen.

The next morning, as I lay on my hospital bed, my movement being minimal as my body healed from the shots, breaking news erupted on the BBC news at noon: Prominent InnoFuel's CEO, Eric Leighton found his wife, Joan found dead in her sleep. Her death was being treated as not being suspicious and that she had passed away in her sleep.

'Eric, what have you done, you coward? Am coming to you, whatever, you do! Am coming for you!'

Almost immediately a nurse came on with a note saying it was handed by a gentleman at the reception. I opened it and it read:

'Len, we know what you are thinking. Do not attempt to fly to New York, it is a trap. We cannot protect you if you leave Britain, our hands are tied. Regards, S & D.'

My mind was made up, I had to do the right thing. Having survived five years in the harshest of wars, I felt ready.

044 – Joan's deliverance

'Dear Len, I am so happy to know you are back, alive far from when we gave you up for dead. This letter reaches you by the night before I am sure to die. I had to write to you and have this delivered through Josh's email address. Eric probably has my emails, phone calls scanned, possibly placed cameras I don't know of. Am probably some spying surveillance officer's wet dream, who knows?

It would have been a lot more exciting had it not been because Eric is paranoid and does not trust me. After all that I did for him, would you believe it? You knew, though I wouldn't tell you of why I left InnoFuel when things seemed to get better and better for me. It's all a big lie at the top, the view from there is frightening. I was a cog in the wheel that dug its feet deep where it found oil. Len, we have been orchestrating terror, death and destruction in every part of the world where there was a pot of black gold to be had.

I saw Eric turn from the one I loved to one I was afraid of, so I left. I am worried sick of Josh, Len. Knowing Eric, I know what is coming and this is the bitter end for me. I am free, I cannot live these lies anymore, feels a lot better with no guilt in my heart. I don't think I will be allowed to live much longer, Len. I wanted to ask you of Sara and your son but I won't make it beyond a few days from now. Josh is growing up just as your son, though your God son is a lot older and mature. Josh knows about Eric and he is confused about his father.

I want Josh to decide on his own what he chooses to do, he has his mother's clear of sense of right and wrong. Meet him if you can as the circle of lies would unwind after they deal with me, tell him the truth: his mother has and will always love him, watch over him for what is best for him.

I cannot imagine what you have gone through all these years and Sara's fate will remain unknown to me. Please forgive us for what we have put you through. You're coming back from almost certain death gives me hope. Tell the world, Len. Tell them if they wish to listen to you and change. Don't believe their lies but try and tell them the truth, maybe they will listen.

Regards,
Joan.'

My hands trembled as I read the email on my inbox on a phone given by Sam and Dave earlier. Cold, isolated and defeated, I looked up at the television as breaking news unfolded on the morning news.

It was exactly as she had envisaged: Innofuel linked her to the decision of sending me to the Golan Heights. Eric had another body as a stepping stone across the bloodied cesspool of lies. We were stepping stones for him to his land of Eden.

'But not you, Josh, not Omar. You are the future and this is why I am here to meet you. To tell you the truth of your mother's sacrifice, to tell you the truth of your God mother's sacrifice, all

220

for nothing but the love for their sons. That's why I asked you to meet me in the record store, Josh. The world may sugar coat a few candies but there is plenty of bitterness out there from which we make all these in different shapes and colours. You needed to know where all these lies about your mother were coming from, the answer was right there in your email. Joan wanted you to decide on your own what to do with it. That's why I am here, to tell you the truth.'

Josh was a fine young teen I thought as I looked at him: unsure of what I had just told him. Joan had quite clearly said not to far from the truth and I had to respect her last wishes. She and Sara were the same in many ways, it was Joan who had introduced them together on one of Eric's lavish parties. Two strong women whom I knew and loved dearly were lost, I had much to do.

Josh sensed my isolation as I was lost in thought. The entire story from my point of view of the last few years had a profound effect on him.

'Would you have my father behind bars?'

'No, Josh. It is your mother's wish to let you decide, I understand and respect that. If not for your mother, I would have never had a wonderful wife and son! I respect her wishes, this is not for me to take. It is yours.'

I gave Josh a hug, I had to go. I had hoped to meet Joan instead of reading her letter to her only surviving son. Oh, Mahmud, were you here you would give me counsel with Sara whose fate seemed sealed within the troubled lands to which return seemed impossible.

Little did I realise that Josh had already left quietly. I didn't get to bid him farewell as he left as if looking for something that had already found him.

Walking through the streets of New York, bustling with activity with people walking around like Egyptian kings past singing troubadours and street performers. Life was a contrast in colour, a far cry from the dust and desolate yellow in the Arabic dessert. The contrast brought a tear to my eye and I had to sit down by the side of the road as the sun set across the Manhattan skyline. Why did you create such myriad contrasts of joy, pain, relief and love across this canvas of both hope and despair? What is your plan then, when all else hurtle towards the painful inevitable end as some pretend to enjoy the moment and love to live now? What is your plan then, I asked looking up above at the darkening skyline. No rockets would pound this skyline, no children would be lying dead around the streets, and no one accused shall be beheaded in front of a blood thirsty mob. Yet, the other side exists in a world I know.

I questioned God's plan as I looked up into the sky. Our karma would come back, all in good time.

045 - Proud and Desolate

I felt a strange homecoming entering the reception of the massive facade of the InnoFuel building the next morning. That strange feeling of homecoming with the family missing as no one awaits to greet you yet the feeling of familiarity is overwhelming.

I had met Eric here for the first time after applying for my dream assignment of being a geological survey engineer of this exciting multi-national group. There on the right, the black and red plush sofas where I would wait anxiously, keeping my calm before the interview. I was to meet Eric and Brian at the tenth floor suite and I remember Sara's wise words of assurance: remember, you are there to collaborate, that's important you know that it is a partnership, an association that would benefit both sides.

Her words were excellent advice as I realised during my interview. Eric and Brian didn't just need another work horse, they needed a go-getter, someone who could scale his work and improve and improvise as he went along. I fit the bill perfectly and the space Eric gave me in my work only made my assignments more successful. It was perfect, almost too perfect.

'Sir, Can I help you? Whom are you to meet today?'

The bright faced receptionist broke my reverie as I collected my thoughts.

'Oh, sorry. Am here to meet Eric, SVP Innofuel at the 10th floor Suite please.'

'Am sorry Sir, do you have an appointment? Mr. Eric does not meet without an appointment. What is your name, Sir?'

'My name is Len. I used to work for Innofuel for the best part of a decade. Eric has known me for that long, you will know when you mention my name.'

'Please take a seat, Sir. Let me call Mr. Eric at his office.'

I just know where to sit: same place on the far right as I did on my first interview. The memory of those years brought a weight on to my walk, so much had changed over the years: one took the path the path of darkness, the other struggling to stay in the light.

Eric was not the man I knew when I first met him. He was ambitious but ruthlessness built on him over the years much like the blood of a human turns a tiger's taste. Eric got deeper into Innofuel's inner circle as I struggled to keep up on the outside. Our work and interpersonal dynamic was perfect up to point when our social meetings started. Eric was enamoured of Sara when he first met us in a celebration right here in this building's rooftop in a party.

Much to his wife, Joan, an amiable and beautiful young woman who was disappointed with her husband's seemingly harmless flirting. I was surprised and taken off-guard by this dynamic but Joan, that beacon of hope kept us at ease always. She was the very 'public' face of the company at the time, always putting her positivity on InnoFuel's 'greener' initiatives and she adored both of us, so much that we became Josh's God parents.

'Len, I was expecting to see you, yet I cannot say I was looking forward to it.'

I turned around to find Eric, or what seemed to be an apparition of Eric standing before me. Before me was what appeared to me to be the unhappiest man on earth I knew. Eric had lost weight significantly, his gaunt face appeared to have had no rest for days. Suddenly, all my anger disappeared as I stood before this man who was nothing but a sorry sight.

'Eric, so nice upto the point of just seeing you now. Guess, I don't have to ask how you are? You look like you have kept better.'

'Are you here to destroy me?'

'Eric, I have no guns, knives or needles to kill you with. I hadn't planned on killing you or destroying you. I have lost myself for years now, lost Sara in the desert, barely managed to bring my son back from sure death. I am just tired, Eric. I just came here to ask you one question: you knew the risks, yet knowing we were close like family and friends; why me? Why us?'

'Why not you, Len? Seeing you and Sara together I had realised that night when I met Sara for the first time: with all the money, power and influence in the world there were some matters that I could never win over.

It just seemed appropriate to fill that seeming weakness with layers of more influence in powerful circles to a point where I wouldn't care anymore, where you or Sara or even Joan wouldn't matter anymore.'

'Eric, Sara was my life buoy and a guiding light for a worn out conscience! You broke her, Eric, you broke Joan! Try living with that. She was a shining diamond, a pity you should have had no place around her!'

'You are probably right: the grass is greener from farther away I suppose. But to all this that effected the change in me, it was you that I blame. Somehow I wish I had never met a content shepherd like you right here at this very spot fifteen years ago. Guess I will have to live with it now, alone!'

'So this is about Sara? And you are blaming me?! Eric, I remember what you were like when you hired me. Come back. Even I should hate you, I don't. You need to stop now.'

'Know this, Len: having seen what has happened I would not change a single decision of my past and that includes when I decided to place you in that fateful assignment. I don't regret sending you there if that's what you needed to know. Now I have urgent matters to attend to, good bye, old friend!'

'He knows!' I spoke out aloud, hoping to help my once friend and mentor back on a path to recovery: I could still save Eric, if he let me.
As Eric turned, my revelation startled him. I didn't wait any longer to tell him further as I walked away towards the exit. After speaking with him, I felt my friend was lost in there somewhere,

226

in the grips of a vengeful spirit eating away at his soul. I couldn't bear to look at him much longer.

'Who? Who knows?'

Eric's voice bellowed from the lounge as I headed out into the busy streets of New York. No more, I had tried to get some answers and I had them. But there was one last mission I had to attempt before the cause was lost.

046 - The Martyr

For the length of an hour after Josh had read the email from his sent items he wouldn't move. The world had changed as he knew it, his perception of the ones closest to him would never be the same.

He remembered on the first time ever before he had participated on a school debate, the doubts clouding his mind.

'What if I fail, Mum? I am scared.'

'Scared of what, son? Scared of losing? Scared of the fact that you might not be able to make a point when it meant the most? Remember, Josh, it is fairer let your opponent win if he has a valid point. Trying to respond or make a rebuttal over every point will only diminish your role as a constructive speaker. Now what do you want to be? Just an opposition speaker or rather someone who has a valid point to make when none exist?

His mum's words rang in his ears, as hot tears fell down his shirt as his knees felt close to collapsing. The thought of her being gone forever had taken time to sink in. To realise that she had not died naturally brought bolts of pain and agony into the boy's mind and heart.

Throughout his childhood, Josh had never had spent enough time with Eric as the senior submerged himself further into his work. Despite living under the same roof, Eric was always gone in the morning when he had breakfast and did not return until late after he was asleep.

Most of his hours besides school was spent with Joan and at times Sara when she visited the house.

Josh was proud of her mum, more than ever now as he realised the extent of her sacrifice in bringing him up as a normal child when every moment in her own life was a seething lie.

'I cannot let mum down, she would be proud of me if I did something worthwhile in my life for a change. She would hug me and all my worries would disappear.'

He remembered and now felt a twinge of anguish in his heart as he realised there was absolutely no one in his life that mattered. Clutching at his mother's clothes, he lay down and closed his eyes trying to feel his mom around him. It worked for a while but the anxiety and anguish came back to him even more till it became unbearable.

'Mum sent this mail from my email for a reason. She wants the whole world to know, this is what she wanted.'

He took the email as a picture and posted it to both Facebook and his Twitter accounts. He captioned it with the words: My Mum's last words, she didn't die a natural death. She died for a reason. The reason was to let the world know of the truth. The truth behind sending a man to die, about greed and the one person behind it: my father.'

In a fit of rage, he went down to his father's bedroom and took his antique Smith and Wesson from his safe, whose combination he knew.

It was loaded with a single bullet.

'Josh, are you home?' Eric had reached home as he entered he found his bedroom door open.

'Yes, am here. Am here, Dad. Come in!'

Eric saw the gun in his son's hand. The sight terrified him and he almost hated himself for acquiring the antique from a senator who had met him earlier this month to finalise another trade deal in the Middle East. The gun was a gift but in Josh's hands it was a weapon.

'Son, put the gun down, easy. What are you doing?'

'You tricked us. You tricked us, Dad. I am proud of Mum but I just hate you so much right now. You hated me, you hated mum, why did you have me? Why?'

'Son, what are you talking about? Just please put the gun down, Josh. Then we will talk.'

'Mum told me everything and I have posted her email on Facebook and Twitter. You are going to jail, do you understand, you scumbag?'

Eric realised but froze as he thought of getting his online accounts and remove all traces of evidence his departed wife might have kept. But the situation here was delicate, what was in his son's mind? Was Josh trying to kill him?

'I am proud of Mum, proud of what she has done. You never did love me, did you? I have now told everyone of who you really are and instead of being forced or bullied by you or your power, I will now go to mum, I can see her waiting for me.'

Tears dropped off Josh's cheeks, before Eric realised a shot was fired. The echo of the Smith and Wesson revolver echoed through the house as Eric screamed. The bright walls splattered with blood, the unmistakeable aftermath of a shot fired with intent, perhaps with intent, perhaps not.

Eric looked on as he fell on the floor, he felt his life slip away as the blood swept across the floor, towards his face, kissing his cheek. It was over, the worst of it, for better or for worse though neither had seen it coming.

048 - Curtains for Sam and Dave

'Am afraid this is a dead end. For both of you, am afraid.'

Sam was defiant in the face of his career being sentenced an untimely termination. Not surprisingly, the British media had not been sympathetic to his disclosure and subsequent actions after they were made public.
There were pages devoted to his deviation from his 'duties' in getting directly involved in what was a 'state matter'. There were a few who wrote differently though:
Sam and Dave had acted on a human instinct in trying to bring me back safe what was perceived as a lost cause: an unsuspecting pawn in a power game, a nameless player who had morphed into a different human being to survive with undeniable hope and managed to come back home with a future in form of his son.
Sadly, this gave the tabloids, sensationalists and the Left endless fodder to use my life's challenging twists of fate as a case study for the lost cause of refugee migration.

'Am still here, still alive. How can you speak of me as if I was a fact on a page in a history book?'
I wanted to scream out to those who would care to listen.

Dave, however, couldn't take this lying down. Looking at the judicial tribunal, he scoffed.

'There is no limit to your hypocrisy, sirs. You condemn us in attempting to rescue a man perceived dead along with his wife. One who managed not only to survive but just wanted to move along with hope and love, tried to integrate with the locals. Not only did he succeed but also had a son even when all hope of returning back home seemed bleak. As if that wasn't enough, he lost his family but came back from the dead to find them. We could not recover his wife from the army's generals. The least we could do was to extract him out of there!'

'Dave, he may be a hero in the eyes of the common people, they are probably planning a book and film deal for him right now. But he is a living expose of the Western world's involvement in the politics in the Middle East. An embarrassing expose to America's greed in rolling the war machine for its own profits. They have had their share of grief in Snowden. Now Britain is being seen as harbouring a vigilante civilian and that weakens them and us even further. It will not do, we will deal with Len soon. But we will have to let you go gentlemen! You will receive a formal gag order on your desks. Nothing, no information is to be made public beyond these doors. You are both excused.'

The sentencing was complete. Sam and Dave were rolled off without a state pension and a gag order meant they couldn't share or protest with the rest of the world. However, that didn't stop them from making a call to me from a phone booth.

'That's it, Len. We are done and having done our job, we are to retire without state pensions. No jobs, no one would be willing to hire us considering all the press we have got in this delicate matter.'

'What about Omar, Sam? Will he be ok and have a future here in Britain?'

'He will be safe here, the government has agreed to help with his schooling until graduation. He is a bright kid, your boy: the scholarship trials were no challenge for him. But you will have to keep moving, Len. There aren't many places to go or hide for you but I would say keep moving, let no one find you at one address. Dave and I have been paper pushers in that department and we know exactly how it works. You can stay a step ahead if you keep moving, ok? '

Sam's words meant I couldn't be with Omar all the time. Ironic as it may seem, though we were out of the danger zone, I would have to stay on alert and live as a nomad. The struggle wasn't over.

'Len, it's Dave here, I know how you are feeling about this. We aren't supposed to tell you but you are not safe here in London, or even in the UK. Pentagon's pretty mad at your expose and they will have little choice but to hand you over for questioning. From then on, it could be as bad as spending time in Guantanamo. We did what we thought was the right thing to do, I can speak for both of us that we are proud we did it. Leave aside all the public slander the government has heaped on us, but we will live. You, my friend, will need to move around if you wish to keep living.'

I thanked them both for what they had done. If it were not for them I wouldn't be here telling my story to the ones who wanted to know the truth.

Sadly, among those were film and book producers as they wanted to publish my disclosure for profit. I gave them my story for little, just enough to ensure it all went into a savings trust for Omar's future.

Reliving the horrific moments was a pain, as I sat by the ghost writer's desk recalling my story. The screams of the men being slowly beheaded on the city center still haunt me. As their screams die out with their wind pipes torn, I felt my own screams silently vibrate within me.

The market terrace, full of kids and adults alike, the kids as young as 5 years old. They would just stand there looking at the spectacle of the young Sunni boys getting beheaded in front of them. As the head and the body departed from each other, the crimson on the ground grew thicker, brighter. The bodies piled on into an untidy heap at one end, the dismembered heads on the other end. Ten executions one day and that was it for the afternoon. The kids went back to their homes with the executions firmly ingrained into their psyche.

My account of these events left the ghost writer stunned. We never report this, we never show this to the whole world. We thought this barbarism was over centuries ago and that the world fights its battles with bullets, guns, missiles and modern machinery. Wrong. It is still fought with a sharp knife, a sword, stones and axes. We haven't evolved much as we thought or would have liked to believe.

Strangely, living now in the free world, the seemingly normal life of the city just made those recollections worse. I felt like I didn't belong here anymore, that I must belong somewhere else. The source. The source that changed me is the key, so I must go back to the source to find my peace when none of the pleasures of modern living gave me any succour.

There was only one conclusion to make, to close an unfinished one. That meant going back for Sara one last time, now that Omar's future was set in a manner both of us would have wanted.

I had to go back, I had to know what happened to Sara. Sara who held on to hope when no one else did, who loved and trusted when it would have been impossible to do either, who raised our Omar against all odds. I had to close that page in my life even if it were my last.
The war zone had changed us but sadly, the war zone remained my only hope and the only place to call home.

049 - The long letter to Omar

Omar hadn't seen me for more than a week since I had gone to the city to meet Sam and Dave. When he met me at the school premises, he ran towards me and we hugged each other. From his hug I knew the one question he wouldn't ask: what about mum?

'Omar, I have a letter for you, something I want you to read this weekend, not before, okay?'

Omar looked at the letter and then at me.

'What is this? Dad, what are you going to do?'

Omar saw purpose and intent in the letter, vaguely understanding its purpose though he wasn't prepared for it.

'You will see when you open it. Tell me, how is the school and the hostel warden treating you?'

'They are very nice to me, but I was wondering when are we going to stay together? Wouldn't you tell me about Mahmud Nasser and village where I was born?'

His questions involuntarily caused my eyes to turn moist. It was true, we had hardly spent much time together and we had already lost being with each other while he grew up. Omar felt truly relieved that he did indeed have a father and that his father had saved him, though nearly had succeeded to save his mother. It was this question, the unasked one, the one that was still unanswered: what about mum?

'Omar, you already know about Mahmud when you met him! He is a lion at heart, the brave warrior that you saw in him at the Gokmuksa village. There will be time to tell you all his stories today. I will going away for a while tomorrow though.'

'Where are you going?'
Omar's eyes seemed to hope for the answer he wanted.

'Am going back for mummy, Omar.'
'You might die, how do you plan on getting back?'
'Am only planning yet to go there and find her. I must find her, my son before I lose her again forever!'

Omar's eyes clouded and he hugged me. It was a tough decision but he understood the choice, hoping both of us could come back together at some time.
'I want to come with you too.'
'Not a chance in this life, Omar. You will stay here to continue your education. Your mother and father has survived many conflicts, don't worry about us, we will always be there for you!'

With this Omar's eyes lightened up and we swapped stories of his first few days in the boarding school, his first few 'English' meals and his new pals. Through his accounts, I felt as having lived as a school boy again, with fresh ideas, ignorant of the inevitably vain and vile nature of this world. We just could not stop laughing for hours until it was time for me to go as the hostel warden gently called Omar to fall back for bed time. It was time for me to leave for my final journey.

Besides writing on maintaining the basic etiquettes of behaviour at school, I had to pen in a few facts that could have served well on a letter if he was older. But both of us were running out of time, so I had written among other things this one prayer:

'Omar, while you grow up in this lovely sheltered part of the world, I want you to keep in your prayers those whom we have left behind. Not in Gokmuksa where I found you but in another remote village where you were born.
Keep in your nightly prayers to ask God to give a special kiss to Humzaa, the boy who lost his entire lower jaw while standing close to his father defusing an IED. May God bless his soul as he tried to live and survive in his dazed state in the makeshift hospital at Qatmah.
Always have in your prayers Noor, Ali and Fakher. They were your friends in Qatmah who died after our village was attacked by a chemical gas released by the army. You were too small but we had to hose you and the other children down as the chemical burnt into your delicate skin and you had stopped breathing for a minute. Your friends could not make it though I tried.
Remember Javed, who was like an elder brother to you when you were just a baby. He was shot in the head then blown away as he tried to help his baby sister escape rebel fire. Keep them both in your prayers.
But most importantly, Omar, and I ask you of just one action: Forgiveness.

Pray for those who had fallen around you, forgive those who made them fall around you. Conflict does not make a man, my dear son. Dealing with the conflict does, and that is what you are going to do in this life.

First, you must win the conflict within you. I know it is difficult, I still have trouble forgiving myself for what has happened and at times for what I had done to survive. If you can forgive yourself, you can free yourself of these horrors.

Once you win this conflict, only then attempt to win over others, not with force but with your heart. You have Sara's heart, Omar, make her proud and I hope we can all be together forever one day.
You will hear from me or of me soon. Do not believe everything they would say about me in the news, just remember why I am leaving.
I will keep my promise, I am assuring you this my dear son. Be good.

Love Always,
Your father.

050 – One Final Try

'And we have reports coming in from our Middle East borough of a possible missile attack on a Syrian airbase reportedly sanctioned by the United States of America. The air strike is being seen as a direct response to the Syrian dictator's barbaric attack on its own people at the village of Idlib.'

Waking up to the breaking news early morning I landed in London with my mind made up. I was late once again to go back for Sara or did this say something about me? I felt a slight twinge of unease, as the angina played up in my heart. The condition had taken over me gradually over the period of time after the abduction at Qatmah, a slow feeling of unease as doubt seeded my being as I had sized up the enormity of my mission then. Then what about the enormity now?

Too much pressure on my veins, my war ravaged psyche was showing the cracks, unsympathetic to my age: I was touching forty. Five years in the belly of the devil is more than enough to spin one's sanity many times over. Only hope could help me try and live through to my natural conclusion, finding Sara and bring her back safe. There in the mission was a paradox, bring her back to here? Where is here?

'Did you know?'

I asked Sam over a public telephone. Sam had forfeited his career to have me rescued from sure death yet he still felt an empathy towards me. We spoke over public telephones for his fear of being bugged. Sam had become increasingly paranoid ever since he and Dave were relieved of their jobs, let out loose on the streets of London for the hounds of the enemy to pounce on them. Without the protective shield of the secret services, his half measures of not choosing a side had already claimed Dave.

Just a week after being relieved of his duties, Dave was found lifeless with no signs of external or internal injury yet was not treated as a suspicious death. A side had to be chosen, should Sam go rogue and join the other end of the secret services spectrum his days as a free man were over.

'Yes, a few hours before the launch began. We didn't join in, couldn't move in without a public session at the Commons anyway.'

'How long before we have a full air strike across the country, not just air fields? Just a matter of time before a communist counter-strike turns rubble to dust around every inhabitable piece of that country? It won't just stop there either, this time it's our streets, that's where the war will be.'

I closed my eyes, trying to shut off the image of total pandemonium on the streets with Russian nuclear fallout contaminating the streets of London. Forget every moment that you cherished, every one whom you loved, what you found in abundance was about to get limited in supply.

'Len, we took a great cost in extracting you from there. Think of Dave's sacrifice, should that be in vain?'

Trying my best to keep my voice steady, my being shook as I decided once for all the inevitable decision I was delaying.

'Dave would have wanted me to make that journey, it would be his last wish should he knew. I am going in, Sam.'

'There will be no extraction this time, you know that. You won't be able to come back by the borders either. This time it is a one way street.'

The angina in my heart was getting worse, I could fully comprehend what Sam meant. He was a realist but what were the odd on me for surviving in the war's epicentre for five years? I had to believe that stats didn't apply to me, what other choice did I have? Could I let Sara's last words haunt me forever? No, I cannot give up, cannot give up now. God, just one last try.

The thought kept my heart from giving away, feeling unwell as I did taking the road via multiple bus routes through Europe. I had to avoid being recognized on the cameras on the Eurostar train stations, the best way to do that was via coach. This was the sixth coach I had changed, the last one at Praha.

Life seemed so serene going through Europe but the body needed that surge of adrenaline only found in unnatural circumstances of close proximity warfare. Was I addicted to violence? My mind revolted against this idea but the body just craved the fight or flight feeling I hadn't felt since I fell wounded at the feet of Salem's cohorts.

Tracking the movements of the FSA unit led by Mahmud was not difficult, I hadn't told him that I was about to come into his territory unannounced.

'Should you know, Mahmud Nasser, forgive me for not telling you as I come looking for answers, for Sara. To try and close what I started as a man, on my own.'

My Godfather, may he forgive me on this quest, my last one. I was not sure if I hold a gun steady anymore. I was not sure if I was Len or was I Naim? Did the name matter, who was I?

My thought cleared as I was hustled into a freight boat hold on its way to Cyprus, the safest boat trip back into Turkey. As I huddled with other fearful refugees whose only wish to go back was the same as mine: Family. At that moment, on that boat we were bonded by the one underlying unwritten unspoken pledge we had taken before we stepped on that boat heading back towards the melting pot of the future of the world's cause for a lost conflict now awakened, globalised and speaking to you in so many ways, in your home, in your churches, mosques, temples.

Through the teachings of the rabbis, the holy Quran, the Bible, the modernists, the pacifists, revolutionaries, the elitists, the politicians and the whole lot of lying wordsmiths: the change was coming, threatening and knocking at your door, while we slept, got lazy and kept our sincere well-meant promises pending for tomorrow. The other end of the spectrum was finally shading the world in darker inevitable shades.

We are just ahead of you, not behind you, not lost at sea, but at home where we are and where we are to go. Does anyone ever wonder what would happen if the world as we know it just went up in a blaze, in a brilliant flash of a nuclear explosion? No one can know for sure but those in another galaxy, a thousand light years away will see a brilliant flash in their night sky, oblivious of our existence. Wouldn't it be too late to call out for help? Would the call be in vain as those would behold the light would scarcely understand our plight?

I felt Sara's warmth close to me almost as if she were here, making this treacherous journey back to the hellish underbelly of civil war. May God help us as we come back for our loved ones, our families to walk across that treacherous border into the hell fire of war stricken land?

Lands set on fire by greed and the lust for power. Lofty words passing judgements on decisions taken by powerful men of the world. I was just going for the one soul that meant my life to me. I am coming for you, Sara. I am not letting you go, in this life or the next. They cannot keep you far away from me, in the heavens, in the oceans under the earth or in the beyond. Where you are I will follow as you did follow me because you loved me. I can never give up on you, Len loves you and so does Naim. Who can keep us apart if there is so much love just waiting to be united? Even the Gods would conspire to bring this love closer. Amen.